BEYOND
STEAMPUNK

Published by Old Sins
Knoxville, Tennessee 37922

Cover and interior design by Luna Creative, lunacreates.com

Trade paperback ISBN: 9780991590186
Ebook paperback ISBN: 9780991590193

For Cordelia and her late nights pulling this together.

TABLE OF CONTENTS

INTRODUCTION

In 2016, I was asked to be part of a panel at Dragon*Con called "Beyond Victorianism". It was part of the Alternate History track and was intended to be an examination of the less explored realm of alternate history. After the fact, I got the feeling that we were supposed to explore existing works, like those of Marion Bradley, Stirling, de Camp, and others. Instead, the panel organizer, Barakha Guggenheim, the other panelists, and I examined jumping off points for stories, ones that were untouched or only lightly looked at in the literature. For example, Ms. Guggenheim and I explored the fact that the Dark Ages never actually happened, and the Early Middle Ages (as they are now known) were a time of scientific, artistic, and cultural sophistication and advancement.

As a panel, we explored the Mediterranean civilizations, the grand African empires, underlooked Asian civilizations, and so on. We decided, then and there, to create an anthology devoted to fantasy and science fiction based around lesser explored history. We would ban the commonplace, such as pretty much all of English history, the Roman state from 80 BC to 300 AD, the American Civil War, Feudal Japan, and so on. All of those have been done to death, and, while they had many more stories to be told and a lot of great work in the field, we felt there needed to be an alternative alternative history.

This anthology before you is the result, and hopefully there will be more to come. We have fantasy, science fiction, and myth, from some well-known venues, like France under the Sun King, to the obscure, like Croatia in the second millenium BC. We hope you enjoy the stories as much as I have putting them together.

Joseph Cadotte
February, 2018

(unfixed in time)

THE EPISTOLARY HISTORY
Alex Shvartsman

#1

1/9/12

Hey Cat,

We finally did it! The time machine works. The blokes are talking about trying to sell it to some big technology company, but I have a better idea.

A quick and easy trip to grand-grand-grandpa Oskar's machine shop in 1890 Weimar, a couple of sketches and a sample left on his desk, and presto: Oskar invents duct tape and builds a fortune in Germany; enough of it gets passed on to my branch of the family a century later that we don't need any vulture capitalists grabbing the lion's share of the time-travel tech profits. Besides, with a little one on the way we can use the extra dough.

So I'm e-mailing to let you know that I'm staying at Oxford to work on this tonight and might miss dinner. On the bright side, if things work out how I expect them to, we'll be dining on caviar instead of pizza.

#2

September 01, 2012

My Dear Cathy,

Yesterday was the happiest day of my life. I finally perfected my invention, but the news of your pregnancy is a miracle that outshines any achievements of mere science.

I couldn't sleep last night, thinking of the world our son or daughter will be born into. England ravaged by seventy years of total war and the constant Nazi air raids — it's not the sort of place in which I want them to spend their childhood.

With a working prototype of the time machine in hand, I have both the means and the moral responsibility to fix the mistakes of the past. I'm going to travel back to 1930, and kill Hitler.

If all goes well, you'll wake up and read this note in a far better world.

#3

Сентябрь 01, 2012

Dear Katya,

My comrades at the Oxford Universitet and I have finally perfected the device. We're scheduled to present Project "Machina Vremeny" to the Politburo in the morning.

When you shared the great news last night, I couldn't sleep, thinking of the world our children will be born into. I can't stand the thought of them living in constant fear of nuclear annihilation that is hanging over all the free people of Socialist Europe.

I possess the means and the moral authority to prevent seventy years of the Cold War. I'm going to travel back to 1930 and kill Roosevelt.

If all goes well, you'll wake up and read this note in the better world, one where communism has already been achieved.

#7

First day of September in the year of our Lord two thousand and twelve

Dearest Catherine,

I received your kind letter a few days since and am dreadfully sorry that the fertility infusions are not yet working. I direct this letter to you in hope that my own fortuitous developments shall cheer your heart and improve your disposition.

The Chronomat device I've endeavoured to design is finally complete. My lifelong dream of single-handedly defending Her Majesty's Empire against those belligerent ruffians from the American colonies is within my grasp. Two centuries of combating the rebels have sapped our resources and surely delayed technological process. By God, we don't even yet have the steam-powered flying carriage, the invention of which the fictioneers of old have predicted to occur back in the 1970s.

The world would have been a better place had the civilized man never ventured into the Americas, and thence I shall presently activate the Chronomat and use it to prevent Mr. Columbus from undertaking his journey.

By the time this letter reaches you at the clinic, we shall all be living in a better tomorrow.

#14

Haab: 12 Mol. Tzolkin: 10 Muluc

Dear Diary,

Once again, I failed to meet a suitable partner today.

I dragged myself to the drinking hall, but there were few single women there, and none of them interested in my advances. Instead, I found myself drinking alone and listening to a pair of inebriated Maya who were apparently anxious about an impending end of the world.

Their main argument seemed to be that the ancient Christian calendar extended no further than 2012. As if the priests of an extinct Eurasian cult possessed the scientific knowledge to predict some future catastrophe. Absurd!

I went home, alone. I couldn't sleep, lying in bed and imagining what it might be like to invent the means of changing the past. How different would our world be if the Mayan explorers had never arrived at the shores of Europe all those centuries ago? What sort of culture and science could the pale-faced tribes of this continent have developed if they weren't wiped out or subjugated by the superior Western civilization?

We'll never know. Traveling back in time is a silly fantasy I conceived of only due to imbibing too much balchè yesterday evening.

I shall purge such thoughts from my mind, bathe, rest, and prepare myself. Tomorrow I shall go out and try again. Somewhere out there is a woman who is destined to be my soul mate. I haven't met her yet, but I remain an optimist.

What historical period did you choose and what attracted you to it?
The story plays with several historical periods. It starts out at World War II and works its way backward. The final scene of the story—and the one I was building up to—is the alternate timeline where the Maya colonized Europe instead of the other way around.

What did you change and what do you see the fallout from it to be?
At the beginning of the story the character's motivation is basically a get-rick-quick scheme. He wants to create a family fortune by helping his ancestor "invent" duct tape a decade before the product was invented in our timeline. Of course, what he thinks of as a small change has enormous and unforeseen circumstances, resulting with the protagonist's new self inventing the time machine and traveling back with a different set of motivations and with each timeline diverging further and further from ours.

What texts were crucial to your research?
I used various websites to research the Maya calendar, so I could provide the "correct" Maya date to match the date of the other segments of the story. This information is easily accessible online, here's one example:
timeanddate.com/calendar/mayan.html

What is a good introduction to this period?
This National Geographic article is a good place to start if you're looking for fiction or non-fiction books about Maya history and culture:
nationalgeographic.com/travel/best-maya-books/

circa 300,000 to 50,000 BC

SHORN
Caroline Sciriha

Adiam moved away from the precipice. None were coming back. Even the great wings of the stragglers, one-armed Jem and sickly Maia, were now too far away to see.

He treaded back to the cave, bare of all that had made it home, especially the twenty-four individuals that had formed the clan. Only one other had had to stay behind. Eva was sitting by the cave opening, finger-tracing his drawing of her mother on the cave wall. At his approach, she tucked her head beneath her wing.

Squatting by her, Adiam drew her close and ran his fingertips down the curve of her spine.

"How long do we have?" she whispered, her words muffled by the wing blanketing her face.

"They left us some food. Two days—four if we stretch it out."

"They should have taken it all. We'll die anyway."

Adiam turned his gaze to the edge of the crag where he'd stood to watch the clan leave. His mother had been the last to fly off, torn between her duty to the clan and her wish to remain with him. He'd never forget the distress on her face as he stood there unable to join her in the heavens, her enormous wings, radiant and ethereal, flapping to keep her in place. She and the other members of the clan had lit up the sky far brighter than the rising sun.

Leaving them some food had been the only thing his mother could do to give him and Eva some hope of survival. At least for a few more days. Even if the gods permitted them to survive, he'd never see Mother again—the spreading indigo-grey in her wings told its own story. She wouldn't outlive the cold season. But she'd known her duty. She'd lead the clan away from the contamination, away from the blight that had killed so much of their food and mutilated this season's children.

Most of the females had been luckier than her, birthing children too deformed to survive more than a few hours. Only he, Eva, Maia, and Jem had clung to life, despite their abnormalities. So the clan had waited, till Jem's and Maia's wings grew large enough to carry them into the air.

Whether they'd be strong enough to reach land still blessed by the gods was uncertain. But they could try. Unlike him and Eva.

"My mother wanted to give us a chance," Adiam said.

"It would have been kinder to kill us. We're abominations."

"Don't say that." He lifted Eva's wing and peered down at her tear-wet face. "You've got the most beautiful colours of the clan. Your wing—"

Eva's half-sob, half-laugh stopped him. "That's right. My wing—one, not two."

And I have none.

Eva turned her head to look at the drawings behind her. "You shouldn't have drawn me. Or yourself."

Adiam's gaze drifted along the string of charcoal and ash sketches; those of Mother were his favourite and best. "I drew us all because…I want to leave a memory of who we are. If the clan dies…." His voice cracked.

He rose to his feet. "Let's eat."

"I'm not hungry."

Giving in to the darkness before the gods willed it time to do so, was not the clan's way. And it dishonoured Mother's gesture. The gods knew how much even that little food could have helped the rest of the clan keep up its strength on their journey.

Lips pursed, Adiam went to the back of the cave and brought the shell of a large bird's egg filled with the last of the season's berries. "We need our strength. We're leaving, too."

Eva stirred. "What? Where?"

"The valley's green—except where the bit of heaven fell." Adiam ignored Eva's sharp intake of breath. "It's the one place the clan avoided all season. If there's food to be found, it would be there."

"It'll be contaminated. It would—"

"Kill us?" He forced his lips into a grin. "So what do we have to lose?"

"I can't walk that far. And why bother? We're doomed. We should jump off the edge together as I suggested. It'll be quicker."

Adiam shook his head. "Before I die I want to know what damaged us, and why our clan faces annihilation. Come with me, Eva. Please."

The climb down the mountain took seven suns and moons. Eva complained every step, every tumble, but she came. Pebbles, dislodged by their descent, nicked and bruised their skin. Her flaccid wing, as well as loose rocks and mischievous roots did their best to trip them up. They trudged on. Finding the bleached rib of some long-dead animal, Adiam tied it to Eva's wing to support it and lift the trailing end off the ground. It helped, a little.

Their food ran out. They ignored the tremble in their limbs, the hollow within, the blurred sight, and plodded on. Rain turned the ground into a quagmire, caking them in mud. They slipped and skidded down the slope. Raindrops, caught in Eva's wing, helped lessen their thirst. They pushed on. The gradient became less rigid, but the mushy ground provided hiding places for snakes, which forced them to pay even more attention where they placed their feet.

Upon reaching the first sign of vegetation, Eva and Adiam collapsed beneath a tree bearing bright red fruit.

Nothing had ever tasted so sweet.

Which didn't mean it wasn't tainted.

Strength meandering back into his limbs, Adiam stood to trellis leafy branches over their heads. It was shelter of sorts from the rain, but at dawn the next day, they worked their way farther down into the valley.

Food became more plentiful, despite signs of blight gnawing at the shoots and roots of most of the vegetation. The deeper they pushed into the undergrowth, the more signs they met that the contagion had clawed deeper into the foliage. By the third day, the greenery disappeared completely, leaving only a scorched expanse with a scatter of skeletal trees and dead animals.

The gods must have slashed at the land with fire as well as contagion.

"There, look."

Adiam followed the direction of Eva's finger. The sun, shining for the first time in days, reflected off a black shape jutting out of the ground. From the crag near their cave the object had looked like a shard of night sky which the gods had hurled from the heavens. From where they stood now below one of the skeletal trees, the object looked more like an egg.

But Adiam had never seen a creature that made eggs that large or that colour. Nor did eggs shine like a frozen lake in spring. Nor had he ever seen black light. The gods muted the darkness with white fires in the heavens and red-yellow fires on the ground.

Eva seized his arm. "It's the colour of blight," she said.

She was right. Everything the contagion touched became dark and rotten. Even Mother's wings shone less bright because of the blight gnawing at her from within.

The wish to run back into the friendly embrace of green foliage made Adiam hesitate. Perhaps Eva was right—it was well-known that some plants and animals were vicious and best not approached. But he'd come this far to face the enemy, dragging Eva along with him. He couldn't back down now.

"Wait here," he said. Eva should be safe at the edge of the dead land. Even though the trees were bare, they would still provide some shelter from whatever form the enemy took. "If anything happens to me, run back into the vegetation and don't try to help me."

"No!" Eva heaved her flaccid wing over her arm. "You're all that's left of the clan. We face that thing together." She slid her hand into his.

The tension within Adiam splintered. He squeezed her fingers. "Together," he said. Pushing his wingless shoulders back, he stepped out from beneath the blackened branches.

The closer they got to the black shape, the more it seemed like the shell of a huge animal, or its egg.

Adiam tentatively prodded the object. It was smoother than Mother's wing-bones and almost as tall as him. Something etched on it made him squat to dust off the soil and mud.

The raised sketch of a wingless male and female appeared the more mud he scraped off. If a god had sketched it, he was not very skilled. The figures seemed misshapen—their faces stretched, their arms and legs too long for their height.

Or perhaps they represented beings of a very different clan, one that even Mother had never seen the like, although she'd lived much longer than anyone else and knew all those whose caves were as far away as they could fly.

The object shook, moaned.

"Run," Eva shrieked.

She scrambled away, darting towards the burnt trees at the edge of the clearing. But Adiam's legs refused to move. The shell vibrated even more, and groaned and sighed like a creature newly awoken.

Adiam fell to his knees. He couldn't fight off a creature that size. Perhaps it had been created by the gods to destroy all that the contagion had not already killed. He picked up a loose rock lying by his knees. He'd try to gain time for Eva to hide.

Before his eyes the black shell split open. Adiam stood and threw the rock at that widening mouth. It hit an inner shell, which was lighter in colour than the outer one, but just as smooth and clear—like a pool crusted with ice overnight. The clicks and moans stopped as abruptly as they had started, but the creature did not bare teeth or claws or lash out.

Adiam stooped for another rock. Before he could throw it, a jumble of images formed on the inner crust.

The rock in Adiam's fist fell out of his hand. He took a step closer to the open shell and peered inside. It was like spying on another clan as it went about its daily activities.

Tiny creatures moved about in a large cave, its walls smoother than he'd ever seen. And there was so much light, like the sun shone within the cave, yet no fire crackled in any pit that he could see. The males and females moved on legs that were longer than their arms, like the clan's, yet none of these creatures had wings. Nor did their skin glow in the dark as theirs did, lighting up the darkness in their cave as they blessed the rising sun and praised the bounty of the god of light. The creatures' skin was mottled—like a serpent's—but perhaps that was the effect of the contagion because both the males and females covered most of their skin with colourful layers, leaving only their faces and hands bare.

Image replaced image. A mother suckled a child. A father threw an egg (or was it a fruit?) for youngsters to catch. Then a group of serpent people worked together, building the black shell, or one like it. The image faded and another formed showing the egg-shape floating high in an orange-white sky.

So much that was incomprehensible.

The images faded, the creaks and moans sounded as the break in the shell closed, barring him out of the strange caves. Adiam stared at the egg. Perhaps one day that shell would open again to release the creatures. Nothing good could come out of an egg that had already destroyed so much.

He picked up a rock and brought it down hard on the egg. The shell did not crack, nor whine in protest. He hit it again and again, but the rock did not even scratch the egg. He couldn't destroy it. And it was too late, anyway. Perhaps it hadn't been the god of the night that had broken off part of the sky to punish them for some lack of judgement. Some misdemeanour. Serpents had dropped the egg in the clan's valley. Serpent people had destroyed the clan, maybe to populate the valley with their own race.

Adiam glanced back at Eva waiting for him beneath the skeleton trees. He and Eva were still alive, though the creatures had shorn them of their wings and family so that they could only dream of joining the gods in the heavens. Yet the creatures also had no wings and had been powerful enough to destroy a land and its people.

Perhaps the gods had sent a message. It was not yet time for the darkness to claim the clan. After all, when a plant died it fed the earth and new plants grew.

Adiam raced back to Eva, and she drew him to her and held him tight. Together they would begin a new clan, wingless perhaps, but one that would strive to regain the splendour they had lost.

What historical period did you choose and what attracted you to it?
I chose a Genesis story, as my initial question was: What if man's drive to explore other planets to find other life forms would ironically result in the mutation or destruction of life?

What did you change and what do you see the fallout from it to be?
Most people would be familiar with the Adam and Eve story. I took a number of elements from that tale, such as the loss of paradise, the tainted fruit, the snake and rib and reworked them into a situation where the story would become a myth through the passing of time, due to the protagonists' inability to understand what the probe that destroyed their people actually was.

What texts were crucial to your research?
None, really, as I knew the Adam and Eve story well. What I did research was my vague recollection of a probe NASA had sent years ago with an engraved plaque. The following link shows the Pioneer Plaques sent in 1971 and 1972, https://**solarsystem.nasa.gov/galleries/706/pioneer-plaque**

What is a good introduction to this period?
Any text on evolution would be a good introduction, particularly Darwin's idea of natural selection, by which organisms change as a means of adapting to the environment, in order to survive. On a lighter note, even though I hadn't seen the series when I wrote *Shorn,* there are similarities to my story in the way *The Twilight Zone* tackles the subject in the episode *Probe 7, Over and Out.*

circa 1600 BC

NIGHTMARES
Elizabeth Kidder

Marina had been a child when the last nightmare had come to her village. She could still recall the second layer of jasmine salve soaking into her olive skin so she wouldn't burn in the brilliance of the setting sun. The sand underfoot was hot enough to turn to glass, but she and the other children's feet were already callused and hardened by years of living barefoot. She and other children from the village gathered most fire-filled evenings before the evening meal to play and practice their swimming in the shallows. Only the few elder boys could go very far, but Marina, wishing for something to fill the small basket she had woven just this afternoon, undid the ties on her skirt to allow the fabric to fall in two sections around her knees and walked boldly into the water.

The ocean was still, the only ripples on its surface emanating from her small strokes and the occasional cresting fish fin. She swam past the last of the boys and stopped, treading water, to look down at the depths below her. The sunlight, reflected on the surface of the still water, amplified and stretched down through the water, revealing layers and levels of fish, sole and perch, flashing smelt and flocks of tunny, eels and stingrays rollicking on the sandy bed, each as clear as if they were only a finger's reach below her nose, encased in rippling glass. She heard a few of the boys calling out to her, but she was focused far below at the litter of shells collected on the sand. Once vacated, not many shells made it to the shallows, tending to collect in the deeper valleys on the ocean floor, and like the other children, she valued each shining shell she managed to acquire. She was a fairly good swimmer, despite her young age, and though she had never attempted a dive any deeper than her own height, she did not fear the ocean any more than a traveler would fear an open plain. that was not on her mind as she took a deep breath and sank below the water.

Farther and farther she sank in silence, eyes wide as the fish danced around her, schools opening and swallowing and spitting her out before they continued on their way. Bubbles slipped from her lips, and she imagined them popping on the surface and releasing the words she was thinking. One particular shell called to her, strangely colorless among the vibrant shades around it. But her lungs were already empty, no closer to the seabed than before, and she scrambled back to the surface, arms wheeling as she gasped for breath. One of the boys, an elder brother from the family that lived beside her own, was already almost to her, and he offered to help her back to shore, which she accepted with the humility and embarrassment of the young when confronted with their own adolescence. She sat in the shallows, keeping cool as the sun sank below the smooth surface of the water, contemplating how many more days she would have to practice before she could attempt such a dive. The elder boys finally swam back in, opening a small sack and pouring out the shells they had gathered, which the other children crowded around excitedly for a peek. Still self-conscious of her failure, she stared determinedly at her feet sinking into the sand, until a shadow fell on her and she looked up to see the elder brother holding out his hand to her. She held out her own, and he placed something in it with a smile before heading back to his friends. She stared down at the shell, transfixed by the hazy grey patina, fading into transparency near its edges. It seemed more cloud than shell, perfectly rounded as it spiraled with a slight silver ridge towards its center.

When she woke up the next morning, the boy was already dead. She tried to give the shell to the younger brother for comfort, but he, aged suddenly by tragedy, knew he would not need it soon, and urged her to keep it in their memory. Within a week the two boys, their parents, and grandmother were all dead. At the family's burial, she wore the shell around her neck, carefully pierced by a woven chain, and had not taken it off since that day.

No one knew where the nightmares had come from, or how long they had been on this earth, but they were not like other beasts. They could not be hunted, captured, tamed, or killed. You might see a darkness on the water that couldn't be leavened, or a restless shadow in the corner of your eye that vanished before you could focus on it. They were as insubstantial as wraiths. The only proof they even existed was their victims, found dead in the morning with bruises on their chests like hoof marks, and hair matted into plaits as inflexible as their stiffening limbs. These tangles of hair were named marelocks, for their resemblance to the wild mountain ponies' manes, and were cut and used as wards against future attacks. The nightmares did not seem to kill for nourishment, or to defend their territory. They were the natural evil of a wild world, with the only certainty being that when a family member was found dead, most often a child, the family would soon follow.

Time passed, and Marina grew into a handsome young woman, dark-skinned with a mass of black curls that glinted in the sun like blood, and after some delicate flirting and necessary maturing, had been joined to Mateo, blond and bleached with eyes that never stopped smiling, even when his mouth had. Together they had a daughter Luna, so named for her hair that shone bright as the moon on the ocean. Marina would brush Luna's hair every morning before weaving it into beautiful silken braids to keep it from tangling in the ocean air. With thirty years since the last attack, Marina did not share the now-legend of the nightmares with her daughter. The children of the village slept peacefully, unaware of the existence of nightmares, kept in the dark by parents afraid to even mention the word for fear of summoning them. But as each year came and went, hope grew that the village would be overlooked indefinitely. No shadows moved in the darkness, and even stories of other attacks in other towns came less and less frequently.

As was custom in coastal towns, Luna learned to swim before she could walk, and when she turned seven, the three of them took their first voyage together across the ocean to one of the many islands dotting the horizon. The winds were with them, and they spent much of the sunlit hours reclining in the catamaran below the shadow of the outstretched sails, reaching a hand down to trail in the water and disturb the beautiful frozen surface between the twin wakes of the boat. Sailing upon the ocean's surface was akin to a bead of mercury gliding frictionless across a mirror, a sharp knife through flesh. Sometimes Luna would shadow Marina at the mast, learning the ropes and rigging of the sails that propelled them forward, or the best way to handle the rudder at the rear. Other times, Mateo would show Luna how to hunt the fish below, whether with patience in catching with string and hook, or the power of a well-thrown spear, and prepping their hauls for meals with the spices they had brought from home. What Marina enjoyed best was their evening meals, licking their fingers clean before Mateo would bring out his tamburica and tell tales, whether retellings of myths or his own stories, often featuring a young moon goddess who rode dolphins through the depths of the sea, which Luna always enjoyed most.

Mateo's playing was what had attracted Marina to him. Most men who had courted her were part of klapas, singing the traditional songs of life and love by the sea, but Mateo had always preferred his instrument to his voice when telling a story. She had come upon him one night, walking along a secluded stretch of beach, playing his tamburica before a small bonfire. Outlined in dancing flames, his silhouette had seemed otherworldly, large and golden, the sounds of the lute weaving notes she could almost see, and then, as he circled the fire, in a soft deep voice he told the story of the Zorja, Morning and Evening Star, guardian goddesses who lived with the Sun on his island paradise. Stories about the Zorja were usually cautionary tales, as they guarded a hound who could devour constellations and so end the universe, but Mateo's story was painfully and joyfully human, telling of the love the Evening Star had for the Morning Star, so much that she chose to press herself into service for all eternity at the Morning Star's side, helping to hold back the doom of the known world. When the song was complete, Marina swept tears from her cheeks and crept away before he saw her. The next day, she found him about to board his fishing boat, and without a word pressed a shell into his hand, a shell she had spent the better part of the evening diving and searching for on the moonlit seabed. It was made of two wings, one bright and bold as day, the other darkly shimmering like stars, both halves fitting together perfectly. She could now see his features clearly in the daylight, the smile in his eyes as he carefully held the shell in his callused fingers. She told him, many years later, that she had come upon him that night, that his song had made her fall in love with him, and he had smiled even more and said that it was fate—he had never played that song before that night.

Watching the way Mateo's fingers flicked up and down the long neck of the lute, so sure of their placement, Luna's face illuminated and haloed in moonlight, Marina wondered if they could sail forever, traveling from island to island, but always returning to the sea, to this beautiful night where the tamburica played and her husband taught their daughter how to tell her own stories.

Luna moved through childhood with grace, not the eager sprint towards adulthood, nor the reluctance to remain in infancy, but content with her age and the singular pleasures it brought—mastering how to hold her breath long enough for the deeper dives to the abalone breeding grounds, playing with the boys her age without fear of tougher emotions than friendship, taking her small skiff on trips to the reefs and sandbars to fish or collect shells. She had great aptitude for weaving, which Marina, herself skilled, gladly encouraged, resulting in an abundance of baskets, mats, fans, and all manner of decorations filling their home, including a special set of patterned weavings that recreated scenes from Mateo's stories, as well as told new stories of her own.

When Luna was twelve, the nightmares came back. A girl, only a few years older than Luna and newly married, was found dead with the hoof-shaped bruises and marelock hair, by her husband returning from an early-morning swim. Terror gripped everyone who was old enough to remember the last attack, while the husband, racked with sadness at the loss of his bride, had to also come to grips with his own mortality as over the next week, both her family and his were taken in the night. He was the last to go, and by the end he seemed perversely happy for it to be over. The marelocks were cut and distributed, the dead were buried, and Marina and Mateo had to explain to Luna the existence of a hitherto unknown monster that could come for them at any time. She took it all in without comment or emotion, but when they went into her room the next morning after a night of restless sleep, they found that she had stayed awake all night, weaving an unbroken chain of martallar bark and marelock hair, using strands of her own shining hair to bind it tighter. They sat down beside her, and after a moment, offered their own strands of hair, yellow and black, which she added to the chain till it circled her entire room.

While the village was numb with shock at the tragedy, there was a black hope in Marina's heart. Never had so many been taken at once. Five had been taken when she was a child, and the nightmares had stayed away for over thirty years. How much longer would they be gone now that nearly a dozen had died? There may not be another nightmare death for the rest of her and Mateo's and Marina's life, and that was enough for her. She felt the shell's small weight around her neck, touched its smooth surface. A lifetime was enough.

Life went on as it had, perhaps more careful and slow than before, but Mateo continued to smile, and Luna turned thirteen, a girl on the cusp of womanhood, and every boy seemed to know it. She kept herself reserved, however, unwilling to show her interest in anything so lurid, focusing instead on her weavings. Over the last year, they had grown more complex, showcasing unique colors made from her own special mixtures of dyes and pigments, and describing more complex scenes. When they travelled across the ocean together, to fish or to simply sail towards the horizon, she began to teach her parents the stories from her weavings, less about man or god, and more about the creatures of the earth, those that stalked the land, flew above, or swam below. She told of the wolf's bravery, the eagle's ferocity, the whale's wisdom, and Marina could see that she would become a great storyteller among their people, able to see the beauty in all things.

But then, one night, Luna came to her parents and asked them to come outside and hear a new story. They sat with their backs to the fire and faces to the ocean, while their daughter stood before them and told a story of a creature of the night, dark and mysterious, who flew on four legs and had eyes bright as stars. Her own eyes gleamed as she said this creature was cursed, unable to stop its actions, causing terror in its wake for reasons not even it understood. Marina felt Mateo begin to shake beside her. She tried to open her mouth, tell Luna to stop this story, but she couldn't breathe, much less speak. Luna held up a new weaving, filled with blackness and shining eyes, and Mateo stood suddenly, racing to his daughter and pining her to his body, holding her softly, but firmly, the dark weaving falling to the ground between them as he, and then she, began to cry. Marina stood too, arms wrapped around her stomach, trying to hold back everything threatening to burst forth. Anger, sadness, fear, but she merely walked over, picked up the weaving, and carefully folded it up till not a speck of black could be seen.

A few mornings later, Marina woke to Mateo's gentle voice suggesting that the three of them go for a sail along the coast.

Looking at her husband, the same smile behind eyes that had a few more wrinkles surrounding them than last year, she knew he too felt the pangs of parenthood encroaching, of loving a thing that was supposed to leave you. They disentangled themselves from each other, got dressed for the day, and began preparing the morning meal, waiting for Luna to come out and join them, to tell her of their plans, eat together, enjoy her for a little while longer. But food sat ready at the table, and she did not, and when they walked to her door and opened it, calmly, because of course nothing was wrong, they did not believe the too-still body, hair matted, the coldness of a room bathed in indifferent sunlight. The weavings rustled in the morning breeze, and she did not, and would not, not ever again, and then Mariana let out a howl that surpassed that of the hound that could swallow constellations whole, for her universe was ending, swiftly and far too slowly.

The elders arrived for the necessary preparations, wrapping Luna in fine linens and bringing her to a back room of the house. There would be no burial yet, not until the whole family had passed, and they advised the two to make whatever final arrangements they wished before leaving without too much haste in their solemn steps. The two sat on the floor, silent, unable to say anything but the occasional guttural sob as the sun rose higher in the sky. Then, around midday, Mariana stood up, retrieved Mateo's tamburica, and placed it in his hands, which slowly moved over the instrument as though he had not played in years, as opposed to last night. He plucked one string, and Mariana, who was not much for singing even on her best day, echoed it. He looked at her, startled, and she looked back, waiting. He strummed another two, and she copied, and then he shifted into the story of the Zorja, and she sang the notes behind him, as steadily as she could, with one hand on his shoulder, the Evening Star behind the Morning Star, forever.

Night fell so fast, and they clung to each other in the darkness, unable to stop the impending doom, offering those meaningless words of comfort and hope, while they silently wished that they would be taken in the night together so one wouldn't have to wake up to the other growing rigid and cold in the morning light. Morning came, and they both woke up, and for a moment it was as though there was no longer any threat at all. Even as cold reality flooded their minds, they were still alive, at least for today, and they spent the day eating their favorite meals, talking, crying, laughing, and enjoying each other in the way of those who know another's body as well as their own. When Mariana woke the next morning, and found her husband cold beside her, she had only two tears left to shed, followed by the cold and hollow dread of the damned. Dark thoughts flooded her as she stood in the center of her home: Should she have told Luna about the nightmares sooner? Should she have known it was coming for them, left the day the young bride died, taken her family somewhere safe? Or would it have followed them, a curse determined and inexhaustible? What if, what if, what if.

Sitting weakly by the open door, watching the sun hover over the placid water, she saw something flutter by the fire pit, and retrieved the still folded weaving her daughter had created of the dark creatures, the nightmares. No longer afraid of the inevitable, she unfolded it with mild curiosity, and noticed that this weaving too had been laced with all their hair, just like the chain around her daughter's room. She clasped it to her chest as the sun rose to its apex and sank again, her last day spent watching the world live on without her. In that sunset, she saw her doom, and she finally stood, going to her daughter's room to lay on her bed, seeing the chain ramble around the ceiling rafters, coiling down into a pile below her left hand, her right still holding the weaving to her chest, and she closed her eyes to the light, not willing to see anymore, to let it come and be done.

Within the dark death of her sleep, she swore she could feel the pressure on her chest, the air escaping her lungs and unable to return, and there was so much of her that welcomed it, knew the inevitability and would not fight it. And yet, within her numb acceptance, there was a fire unwilling, unable, to be snuffed, and once she knew it was there, it roared to life with such fervor that she opened her eyes to get away from the blaze. There, above her, was the nightmare, a creature that had never been seen by human eyes, a being of death, and yet, she was not dead, not yet. She glanced down at where its hooves were planted on her chest, and despite its weight, it was not crushing. The thing stood immobile, perhaps just as shocked as she at being seen.

Her left hand stretched, found the chain, and suddenly she was lightning, escaping from beneath its hooves and binding the creature at its neck. Startled by her actions, it reared, but the chain, mere martallar bark and hair, held firm, and it returned to earth, stamping and snorting. She could now see it more clearly at this distance, shadow given bulk with thunderstorm clouds and black fire hooves, somehow held by the chain in her left hand. Then she remembered what she was clutching in her right, and she held it out to see that though the nightmare had placed its hooves on it, the weaving was not bruised or even wrinkled. The chain, too, held fast, and she was reminded that she had actually caught a nightmare, the very nightmare that had taken her family from her, and within her burned that fire, wanting blood as tribute. But how do you kill a shadow? Where do you land the final blow on a thunderstorm? She had it captive, but that was all she could do, and in fury she harshly yanked at the chain, wishing to at least cause it pain. But it came forward easy now, and suddenly they stood eye to eye, and the brightness of its eyes shone like stars against its inky blackness. Luna had gotten that much right at least. The shine in its eye seemed the same hue as her daughter's hair. Why did it not hurt her to think of her daughter? Sudden exhaustion threatened to capsize her, and as her knees buckled, down went the nightmares head, and though it was only smoke, it pushed her back to standing. It began to walk past her, and she let it lead her by the chain, through her house, out the open front door, down to the shore where their boats floated calmly in the placid water. The nightmare placed one hoof on the still water, then the other, and then it was walking across the surface of the ocean, not even a ripple to mark its passing. She let out the chain, leaned down and untied Luna's skiff, and boarded, both hands holding the chain as it pulled her away from the shore.

They flew across the calm waters. Even the wake of the craft seemed subdued, with the moon reflected perfectly in the mirror of the sea. The nightmare galloped, pulling her and the boat without effort, for what seemed hours. At last, with the moon setting low on the horizon, it slowed and stopped, and Marina saw hundreds, thousands, a sea of nightmares, rolling in like a fog around her. The one she had captured walked up to another, larger nightmare, and the two nuzzled before turning to look back at her. She no longer felt hungry for blood, but neither did she feel scared. The death of her family loomed heavy in her mind. Another came up to her and lowered its head to touch the seashell around her neck with its muzzle. She looked down to see it trot back to a group of nightmares, and she slowly began to see that there were many groups within the herd, some as small as two, some more than twenty. They all had those bright eyes, steady, unblinking, and now the one she had captured and the one it had met were coming back toward her. She thought again of welcoming death, and this time, the fire burned less brightly. She looked into its eyes, and screamed. Those eyes had a smile behind them, unbelievable and all too familiar. She said her husband's name, and it whinnied, a long, low cry. She turned, and said her daughter's name, and the captured nightmare whinnied too. Every name of every nightmare victim came tumbling out of her mouth, and a chorus of neighs echoed throughout the herd, from the boy who had given her the seashell, to the husband whose new bride had died first.

Marina thought again of her daughter's story about the nightmares, cursed things that did not know their actions, and saw that there were no nightmares without death. Her husband, her daughter, the souls of the dead were bound up into cloud and shadow, cursed, or desiring, to bring their families with them. Her family, so many families, stood before her, and when she thought of keeping her daughter restrained so that she might live another day, she knew she would rather die right here then do that horrible deed. For the final time, she thought of accepting death, and the flame inside her quietly burned itself out. She stood up in the craft, steadying herself as she turned to stare across the sea to the shore. The moon had been joined by the morning star, and when she looked down, she could see them both reflected beneath her feet, as though the evening star was now swimming far below. She turned back to the nightmares, and smiled. Then she let go of the chain, and stepped off the side of the boat.

Silence enveloped her as she sank swiftly down, down, past schools of fish that gleamed in the moonlight, followed by swift dolphins, how Luna would have loved to see them, and Marina's thoughts turned back, back to the night after the elder brother had died, drifting to sleep in her childhood bed with a thatch of marelock above her head and her mother singing her an old prayer, as old as nightmares, long forgotten until now.

> Here I am, lying down to sleep;
> no nightmare shall plague me
> until they have swum
> through all the waters that flow upon the earth,
> and counted all stars that appear in the skies.

She looked up at the surface of the water, bubbles of air rolling from her lips, but could no longer see the moon and stars above, for the surface of the water rolled and foamed as she had never seen before, turning the water around her darker and darker. She lowered her head again, and as the last bit of air slipped from her lungs, she saw the nightmares swirling around her, diving into the depths, legs treading water as they attempted to reach her. Her eyes closed, and then she knew no more.

The roaring that woke the townspeople had never been heard before, and they emerged, bleary-eyed in the pre-dawn dim, anxiously awaiting whatever would befall them now. At first, they saw nothing, only heard the roaring, rolling in like a gathering thunderstorm. And then, a sharp-eyed child cried out to look across the water, and they saw them, frothing and frenzied, pounding across the sea with manes of foam and bioluminescent eyes. With cries of terror the people ran inland, as along the shoreline the mares charged, throwing their blue and white bodies against unforgiving sand and rock, only to crash and break, manes caught in the martallar eking out its living on the glistening rocks. They retreated, and returned, pounding in the surf, whinnies and neighs drowned by the rolling of their hooves as they broke upon the shore. Slowly, one by one, the people walked back down to the shore to watch the spectacle as wave after wave of mares, once night and now sea, crashed upon the sand and retreated back into the sea. The once straight line of the ocean now dipped and bumped as the cresting waves stretched out to the horizon. For days, weeks, years after, men would redesign their boats, rethink their fishing and sailing tactics, reshape their views of the world to fit this new ocean that moved without ceasing, and it would be decades before they realized there hadn't been a single nightmare death since the waves had appeared. Throughout it all, the mares continued to swim through all the waters of the earth, forever seeking to escape, forever bound by the water below and the moon above.

What historical period did you choose and what attracted you to it?

Nightmares started out as a myth, one of those ancient stories that explained how the sun rose each day, or the tiger got its stripes. To that end, it had to be set in ancient times, where folklore was gospel, in a region intimately tied to the sea. My research led me to the Minoan eruption, one of the largest volcanic events in Earth's history, which devastated Santorini and whose effects were felt as far away as Egypt. It is further historically important as a fixed point for aligning the entire chronology of the Bronze Age (the second millennium BC) throughout the eastern Mediterranean, and was a perfect event to create a story with worldwide consequences.

What did you change what do you see the fallout from it to be?

Rather than a change occurring from the event to alter our modern world, I instead viewed the eruption as what made our modern world what it is. I reimagined the world, pre-eruption, as a place of living nightmares and silent seas. To me, the stories that explain how we came to be are equally interesting for the world they set up as normal, before the change occurs to make them fit our current interpretation. The correlation between the eruption and the imprisonment of the nightmares was a way to rationalize a natural disaster, and perhaps come to terms with those earth-shattering moments as fixed points in our timeline that may perhaps be for the better.

What texts were crucial to your research?

With the scope of the Minoan eruption well documented, the more necessary research was for the people that inhabited Croatia at that time, as well as their mythology and fairy tales to lend believability to the idea of a new myth. Professor D. L. Ashliman from University of Pittsburgh wrote an extensive paper on the prevalence of the "night mare" across many cultures. The story of the Zorja is lifted from Croatian mythology, and the use of music and instruments was based on the local culture at the time.

What is a good introduction to this period?
If you're interested in the idea of mythology, and would like to see the Zorja again, I recommend Neil Gaiman's *American Gods*. Of course, you can't go wrong with Mythology by Edith Hamilton, the book I was most eager to read for high school English. As far as learning more about the Bronze Age and its historical importance, try *1177 B.C.: The Year Civilization Collapsed* by Eric H. Cline, who also wrote *The Oxford Handbook of the Bronze Age Aegean*.

circa 500 AD

UBAR
Joseph Cadotte

"The sands are coming! The sands are coming," the prophet chanted on his pillar. He was not a Christian, a Jew, or a Zoroastrian. Nor, as his king and so many of citizens did, did he belong to the savage faiths of the local tribes. The god he worshipped was unknown or possibly long dead, but he sat in a nest secured to his pillar in the city of Ubar, and chanted, every day, the same thing.

He was fed by locals and passers-by, by caravaneers who welcomed any blessing. His basket was filled once a day, and then he would draw it up, eat, and, the next morning, send down a pot of offal, and the process would repeat again. He never stopped his chanting, and the visitors from as far away as Hispaniola Ulterior and the island of Lanka observed him, shook their heads, and journeyed onward.

He was not lying about the sands. For three generations, they had come closer and closer to the city of pillars. They had covered the outlying fields and clogged the irrigation ditches. Where goats once grazed, there was nothing but the golden sand. Even so, the way he chanted it, you knew that he wasn't talking about this slow encroachment.

The caravans still came through with regularity. There were still profits to be had coming from Himyar in the southwest to Oman in the northeast. If anything, the growing sands, the Rub al-Khali, made each trip more profitable than the last. So what if the oases were a bit drier each year? There was still more than enough water to quench the city and another besides.

From the pillars, holding up tents that protected the city from the sun, grew green, fruit-bearing vines. Grapes and berries, some of the latter giving sweet dreams or ease from pain, were freely had about them. Water trickled from the pillars, just enough to feed them, with a little besides to turn each pillar into a small fountain. The water gathered into basins at the bottom, and drained away with a burble.

From the top of the pillars, three dozens of cubits up, a mist sprayed into the bright light, landing on the tents, soaking them, with the baking sun moving hot winds over the tents and bringing cool air to the people dwelling beneath them. Even the poorest had rooms in apartments and their own jannah, growing flowers in the shade. Buildings as tall as ever seen in Alexandria or Byzantium poked through them, into the blinding sun.

The sand had, in some ways, become a boon. It could be made into glass, which helped build the new, tall towers, and it could pipe down light without as much of the heat. The sands also meant that more and more traffic had to come through Ubar.

The king, in his own tower, swaddled by spiralling cloth, rippling in the wind, looked over his domain each day at noon, when the light bore straight down into every bit of his domain. Every day, he had his fill of prophets clamoring for his attention, and the one down below chanting about sand was no more a concern than the two who had just left, with their embassy of rabbis, begging him to repent.

The sand still came. The king did not care. He was assured by his priests that the djinn would keep them safe, that princes of air and smoke would repay his people's sacrifices with prosperity. Despite the prophet on his pillar, his nest now collecting grains of sand, he only saw that they had brought him wealth.

His nobles, in their towers (though none higher than his), agreed. When they met with the king, they praised him as if he was already a god himself. When one, who had fallen out of favor, was sacrificed to Athtar, the remaining nobles praised him and even the waters started flowing faster as he built statues of glass and brick to himself and his gods.

Again prophets, this time from Persia, came to him and begged him to repent, and begged him to worship Ahura-Mazda, or the god of Abraham, or even Shiva, but he pointed to the ever-flowing water, and cast them out, killing their servants to drive his point home. The prophet, on his pillar, saw the sand touch it and wrap around its base, and kept up his chanting.

More merchants came, but now they were bringing food to Ubar as they passed through. The grapes were swollen and tasteless, while the other berries drowned. There were no more goatherds, and fresh milk became more and more scarce. The jannah no longer grew flowers but food, and barely enough of that. Yoghurt and cheese became the order of the day, with dried fish, meats, and fruits imported in sealed urns from the coast. Even so, Ubar was awash in wealth. It would not be poverty that brought them down.

The king built higher and higher and more and more. Faster and faster the water surged. It almost did not need pumping, anymore. Each increase came after another noble was sacrificed to another god. Here to Kahil or Athtar, there to an ifrit, or a ghul, or even a lowly jann. Each noble that survived became more fervent in their praise, hoping that he would not be the next to feed the gods, but the king rewarded faith with the same prize as he did those who would betray him. And still the water poured forth. The oases, once half their depth, merged into a lake in the middle of the city.

It was then when the last envoy of prophets, this time from the throne of the Romans in Byzantium, came to him. They met the prophet on the pillar, and like the others, they were bemused by him, but they left an amphora of wine for him, though he had no way to retrieve it from the foot of sand now wreathing his pillar. Like the others, they begged the king to change his path, but he drowned them in a ceremony to Athtar, for there were no nobles left.

When the time for the next sacrifice came, the king sent for the prophet on the pillar. He brought him into his chamber where he had laid out all the tools for the god's feast. Priests were waiting, holding sacred instruments, and the king walked forward to greet him, offering him a chance to plea before him.

"You say that the sands are coming?" the king asked.

"No," the prophet said, "I say the sands have come."

With that the ground beneath the tower, beneath all of the now-empty noble towers, collapsed into empty aquifer beneath them. They shattered into each other, and the tumbling edifices cracked and broke as building after building plummeted into the depths. The pillars collapsed around them, the heavy, water-soaked linen smashing their way down. From the desert, from the land that had once been farmed and grazed, the winds picked up, and they carried the land with them. Rock, once buried, was exposed and buried again, scoured and shaped by flying grit. Ancient brick exploded into more sand which tossed about in the gale, embracing the few pillars still standing, but most following Ubar into the pit. A day and a night of the storm, and nothing could be seen. A day and a night later, the tips of those last pillars saw the moonlight, and a day and a night after that, all that was left was their bare rock cores, chimneys to nothing.

In all the years since, all that can be heard where Ubar once was is the sand shifting in the sun. As the noise echoes from the scorched rock and the broken chimneys, if you are sharp-eared enough, you can hear the wind sing "The sand has come. The sand come. The sand has come."

What historical period did you choose and what attracted you to it?

I chose the time period between the rise of Islam and contraction of the Roman Empire in Arabia. This was a time when shifting climate was changing the face of the peninsula and many settlements were lost. Many of these are the basis for the Lost City motif in much of literature, in sources as diverse as Arabian folktales and HP Lovecraft. Each of these so-called "Atlantis of the Sands" is an inspiration for great stories. Though frequently set in Africa, H. Rider Haggard's novels, such as *She,* are great example of the Lost Civilization subgenre.

What did you change and what do you see the fallout from it to be?

I gave the city-state of Ubar a couple of centuries of progress in architectural and materials technology than it actually had, although, as occurred historically, it was lost before it could really affect anything.

What texts were crucial to your research?

The *Quran* (although there is very little in it about Ubar) and some commentaries. The many civilizations who have destroyed themselves through environmental mismanagement, such as the Maya and the Khmer, or tribes who have done the same thing, such as the people of Rapa Nui. Current archaeological exploration among lost cities, which is made possible by satellites, is another good source.

What is a good introduction to this period?

The Arabian Nights. Even though most of the stories come from places as diverse as Europe, India, and especially China, they are filtered through an Arabian mindset.

circa 500 AD

CALL OF THE KINGUYAKKII
Nemma Wollenfang

"It is the way of our people," Papa said as the aurora reached down, its spectral dance a riot of colour. "Even in eternal slumber, we have our duties to perform."

The gossamer shroud that encased Mama was as white as the powdered snow around it. Atop the mountain that was all there was—blankets upon blankets of it. Her thin veil sparkled where the snowflakes touched, and when the sky shimmers caressed her still form—a feather stroke—her ethereal visage rose up to greet them, ever as lovely as she had been in life.

Little Nuniq clung to her papa's leg. "Will she be alright?"

"She goes to her mother, and her mother's mother, along with all of our ancestors. That is where the Kinguyakkii will carry her." As he spoke, Mama's image merged with the rainbow mass and retreated into the sky. Higher and higher. Behind, stars glittered like mica in the black. He draped an extra fur pelt around her small form. "Together in Tomkin, Home of the Spirits, they will watch over our tribe for all time."

That knowledge did not soothe the ache in her throat. "When will I see her again?"

For that, her papa had no answer. He merely smiled; a sad and cryptic tilt of lips.

Nuniq's mouth wobbled, her breath ghosted. Her tiny hand clutched his leather breeches tighter as an arctic zephyr curled around the peak. "Will she sing me goodnight?"

Papa scooped her up, hugging her close. "I will sing to you, little love."

Through every season the aurora danced and sang. The voices of those who had passed were an accompanying chorus to the everyday hubbub of their tribe. As women gathered to cure seal hides or harvest blubber, as men carved holes through the sea ice to fish or crafted snow into igloos, there were the lights, watching over them. Whenever Nuniq felt sad she would cast her gaze to the ancestor's mountain. Always she'd see them, always they brought some measure of comfort. Her mama was up there; one opalescent phantom amongst the many, another symphonic chord in the gentle hum that sang her to sleep every night.

When Nuniq was one and twenty, she lost a daughter, her first. The babe was born without breath. That same eve her papa was seized with a pain in his chest and strange palpitations.

"I am well," he assured his many concerned tribesmen. "Do not fret."

Soon after, his heart failed.

And so the tribe wrapped them both in gossamer shrouds and carried them to the mountain. The Kinguyakkii was ever-present but always it shone brightest in winter.

Up on the high precipice, where the snow lay thick, Nuniq laid the infant in her papa's protective arms. Blue skin, still lips, both as cold as ice. Her husband helped her move his stiff limbs into place. Papa would care for her babe in Tomkin, just as he had her as she grew.

As if sensing the awaiting travellers, the sky shivered violet and cyan. In a waterfall rush it rippled down—tender fingers of seeking light that came at their shaman's call.

Nuniq stood in her husband's embrace as Papa coalesced before them. Holding the babe, he rose to join the umiak of many faces—too many to discern one from another.

Yet for all their facelessness they sang with familiarity.

And those below sang along with them, their voices rising in a chorus of farewell.

"Take care of them, Mama," Nuniq said.

There was no one left from her youth. Those around her now were all children grown. Many looked familiar—the same eyes, lips, chins on different faces—though she could not recall their names. Only those of the past lingered clearly in her mind now: her first tribesmen.

"Grammy," a boy child said at her elbow, "will Granpy be alright?"

Nuniq cast her gaze to the snow-speckled shroud. Gossamer overlaid his features. The handsomeness of his youth had withered but the love in his eyes had never changed.

"He goes to our forefathers and foremothers," Nuniq said, her wizened voice as hoarse as the glacial wind, "there to watch over us with all of our ancestors, for all time."

Ruby, jade, lilac, and blue—spectral oscillations surged and swelled. The aurora sang with an array of light; a silent melody for the repose of a soul. Young once more, her husband rose and joined the swirling eddies to depart for the heavens. One among the Kinguyakkii.

The boy's lips wobbled. "When will I see him again?"

Nuniq merely smiled; a sad and cryptic tilt of lips—the same Papa had given her when she asked that same question so long ago. Like him, she gave no answer. The boy would understand, eventually. Time was fleeting...

Another came to fetch him, picking him up and carrying him away. The tribe began to disperse, heading back down the mountain to the warm glow of the village below.

Where Nuniq sat, on a low rock perch, she clutched her cane and rubbed her stooped back. Age made her tired, infirmity made her frail, and aches and pains plagued her. That was the curse of the elderly, the price they paid to see the world continue its turning.

"Grandmama, come inside," a nameless young women said. She carefully placed an extra fur pelt around Nuniq's shoulders. "It's freezing out here. You'll catch a chill."

"I will be along shortly, my dear," she said, her eyes on the lingering luminescence.

The traipse of footsteps faded yet still Nuniq remained, as did the lights.

"That's right," she said to the sky. "You've got one more yet."

The rainbow streamers rippled, undulating, reaching down once again. Like a pair of open arms welcoming her home.

What historical period did you choose and what attracted you to it?
Unspecified but pre-colonial. I imagine it to be circa 500 AD. Tribal cultures from any continent have always fascinated me—it's simply the idea of people living back in a time when the world was fresher and freer and possessed a greater air of mystery.

What did you change and what do you see the fallout from it to be?
In *Call of the Kinguyakkii,* the aurora borealis is an almost-entity which plays a major role in the Inuit's afterlife—harvesting and preserving departed souls. This inclusion results in a change to their beliefs and ritualistic behaviour surrounding death.

What texts were crucial to your research?
Some time ago I heard a tale about the Northern Lights and how, in ancient times, they were said to reach down and steal the souls of the living. This sounded like great story fodder, though I didn't know what to do with it. More recently, I saw a TV documentary about Inuit culture, which spurred the story into being. Research on various websites about the native people of Canada helped it along.

What is a good introduction to this period?
Here's a link to the site I used to get a better idea of Inuit culture, perhaps you could use this:
firstpeoplesofcanada.com/fp_groups/fp_inuit1.html

circa 1000 AD

THE TRAVELER AND THE SHE-GHOUL
Eugene L. Morgulis

There once stood a well in the desert, upon which came a thirsty traveler. But when the traveler reached for the water, it receded, and his cup came away empty. He tried again and again, but never could he fill his cup. Not knowing what else to do, the traveler sat next to the well and sang:

> *Cool me and soothe me.*
> *Long is the way, and I am weary.*
> *My throat is parched, but I can still sing songs.*
> *Though I'd sing sweeter with a wet mouth.*

As the traveler sang, the water bubbled up. By the time he finished his song, the wetness overflowed the lip of the well, and he filled his cup. When he had drunk his fill, a she-ghoul emerged from the well. The traveler was pleased to look upon her, for she was beautiful beyond perfection, with skin like a pool on a windless day, and hair like a bubbling stream.

He sang to her:

Bathe me and quench me.
If I drown in you, so it will be.
For when you dry, my life will cease as well.
But today my heart still beats, so let me drink.

Hearing the traveler's song, the she-ghoul pledged her love to him. He took her as his wife and consummated the marriage.

The traveler and his new bride continued on their way through the desert. When he thirsted, the traveler sang to the she-ghoul and she conjured a stream for him to drink. When he hungered, the traveler sang again, and she brought forth fish from the stream to feed him. When a band of ruffians set upon him and tried to ride him down, again the traveler sang to the she-ghoul, and she summoned a wave to wash away the bandits, drowning them and their horses. In this way, the traveler never knew thirst, nor hunger, nor fear.

One day, the she-ghoul said to the traveler, "Why do you keep wandering, my beloved? Better to settle down by the sea, where I shall make you a king."

The traveler did as his wife bade and settled by the sea, where the she-ghoul raised for him a grand palace of sand and coral.

Years passed, and the traveler-now-king grew fat and contented. Wanting for nothing, he forgot what it was to be a traveler who thirsted, and hungered, and feared. In time, he even stopped singing, though sometimes he still hummed to himself without thought or melody.

One night, his she-ghoul wife came to him with shimmering eyes and said, "Oh my husband and king, who was once a traveler that I loved and raised high, you have not sung to me in many years. Let me hear your sweet melodies again, and I shall be grateful."

But the king became angry with his wife and shouted, "How dare you order me to sing like you would a servant? For you, I ended my travels. Now I have no new songs and do not wish to sing. Be gone from my sight!"

Hearing her husband's cruelty, the she-ghoul wept for seven days and seven nights. When she cried out the last of her tears, the she-ghoul dried up and disappeared, taking her magic with her.

The king did not realize what he had done until the palace of sand and coral began to tremble. As archways broke and columns collapsed, the king cried out to no one's ears. He even tried to sing again, but found his throat was as dry as sand. The castle crumbled to the ground, burying him with it for all time.

The she-ghoul returned to her well in the desert to wait for another traveler's song.

What historical period did you choose and what attracted you to it?

I am writing less in a historical period, than in a literary setting, specifically that of the *Arabian Nights* or *1001 Nights*. I researched the *1001 Nights* for a historical novel and fell in love with its type of storytelling. The stories have their own unique logic and are full of humor, action, passion. Many even contain elements of science fiction, centuries before such a genre existed.

What did you change and what do you see the fallout from it to be?

By writing my own *1001 Nights* story, I suppose one could complain that it's non-canonical. However, various versions of the *1001 Nights* collect a multitude of stories from all over—India, Asia and the Middle East—told over hundreds of years. I hope that my story continues in this wide-ranging tradition.

What texts were crucial to your research?

Apart from different versions of the stories themselves, Robert Irwin's *The Arabian Nights* is a terrific companion text that describes how the stories were collected and how translators from differing era's and nationalities have retold them (with varying degrees of success).

What is a good introduction to this period?

You can't beat the stories themselves. I recommend the Husain Haddawy translation.

16th Century AD

THE DEVIL'S BREW
Kelly A. Harmon

Battista Sanservirino dipped his quill in the black ink and scratched a line through the last verse he'd written. Then, he dipped again—gathering great droplets of ink—and scratched out the entire page with a vicious hand, the point of the quill ripping through the delicate paper, the dark ink staining the side of his wrist and the starched cuff of his white linen shirt.

Pushing the carved wooden chair from the desk, he stood and crossed to the hearth. The fire popped and crackled, and he folded the desecrated poem into quarters and shoved it between two burning logs, making certain it would light the first time. As the page browned and curled, and finally caught flame, Battista watched hours of work go up in smoke, the odor of burnt paper signaling his failure.

He put a hand on the mantel, the cool marble a direct contrast to the heat rising up from the paper and stared at the painted miniature of his mother resting beside the free-standing gilt crucifix.

Merda. That was all he could write. *Shit—shit, shit, shit*.

He overturned the painting so his mother would not witness his defeat. Then he sighed, wondering if he should turn the crucifix to the wall, too, wondering if that were a sin—

knowing that the Lord saw everything he did anyway. Why would the Lord not send him a bit of grace? He toiled so hard to be better at his craft.

Battista returned to the table and sat, remembering the words of his idol, Torquatto Tasso and penned the words from Tasso's *Aminta*, Act I, from memory: *S'ei piace, ei lice.*

If it pleases, it is permitted.

It pleased him to write the words of his idol. But it pleased him less than if he could write words as great as those as the wonderful poet himself. And now that Tasso was dead, who would fill his shoes? Who would Pope Clement VIII crown with the laurels?

Me?

Bah. He would settle for finding a patron. For making a living with his art. Then, maybe he could please others.

Battista capped his precious ink, reached for his cloak and his hat, and locked the door of his room behind him. He needed air.

The Gianicolo is *not* one of the fabled Seven Hills of Rome, because of its location west of the Tiber and outside the boundaries of the ancient city, but it *is* where Torquato Tasso planted his famous oak. The summit offered a quiet spot for reflection and was perhaps less traveled to than its famous seven brothers, but most importantly, visiting it made Battista feel closer to his hero. It was there Battista sought his fresher air.

The road to Gianicolo was quiet this morning. Rain kept many away. But it did not deter Battista, it enervated him, the clean air singing in his lungs. He would sit by Tasso's Oak—the one Tasso planted while he waited for Pope Clement to crown him—and meditate on the joys of the verse. Perhaps if he sat where Tasso sat, if he looked at the domes and spires of Rome from the second highest hill in the area, he would see what Tasso had seen. Maybe then he would learn what Tasso had known. He would be able to write like the master.

If I could write a work a tenth the grandeur of Jerusalem Delivered, thought Battista, *I would be happy.*

The hill was steep, the climb hard with no distinct path to walk, and Battista grew faint of breath as he labored to reach the top, stumbling on rocks, and tripping over large clumps of onion grass. But the plain, stout, wooden bench he had paid to have brought here weeks ago remained. And so—breathless—he sat near Tasso's young oak, barely taller than himself, its leaves just budding, and gazed out over the colorful, clay rooftops of Rome.

"If only..." he murmured, breathing in the clean scent of rain-washed air, away from the malodorous stench of Rome, and his troubles—he hoped.

"If only what?" The Moor appeared out of nowhere—and like the pope proclaimed of Moors, his nimble tail would not be still. The barbed tip at the end waved about as though it wanted to shake hands with Battista.

The Moor kept his silky, dark hair swept away from his face and tied in a queue at his nape. And he wore an embroidered vest of red brocade, padded out at the shoulders, and a white pleated collar, which contrasted strongly with his smooth, dark skin. But his pants were tight-fitting, of stringy fur, and his clogs resembled hooves.

Battista looked the Moor over. He was not one to share his business with a stranger, and a Moor at that. But the stranger came closer, bringing with him the faint odor of brimstone, sat beside Battista on his bench and took out a strange flask. The lid became a cup into which he poured a dark, steaming liquid.

"Coffee?" the Moor asked, holding it out to Battista.

Battista could not help himself, he leaned toward the proffered cup with its topping of thick, dark foam, and breathed deeply of the rising steam. The smell alone was heaven, rich and nutty, thick enough to chase away the damp. But he found himself repeating the critics' words aloud. "*Coffee is the bitter invention of Satan.*"

The stranger smiled. "What does it matter who invented a thing, if it is so beneficial to all—so delicious?"

Battista recognized the temptation for what it was, and having acknowledged it, took the cup. It warmed his hands, and he pulled it toward his chest, enjoying the feel of the steam tickling his chin. He sipped. The sweet, hot liquid stung the tip of his tongue, but warmed his gullet on the way down. Dark and rich, the faintest hint of bitter overlaid the sweet.

The Moor poured himself a cup of coffee and Battista thought, *where had the second vessel come from?*

"You're waiting for an audience with Pope Clement," the Moor said, sipping. "Yes?"

He must be confusing me with Tasso, Battista thought. He shook his head. "No. I would love an audience with the pope, but my work is not good enough to reach his attention." He thought of Tasso, whose work was good enough to have reached Pope Clement, and who was told he would have an audience with the pope, and yet sat here waiting for months—until he'd died.

The Moor lifted his cup, nodded over the rim of it, nodded again. He blew across the top of the brew, his breath pushing the foam aside and sending a draught of warm nuttiness in Battista's direction. "Do you like the coffee?"

"Indeed."

"And if you had an audience with the pope, would you tell him of such a brew?"

Battista considered it, but discarded the idea right away. Of course, he *could* talk to the pope about this wonderful drink, but it would defeat his purpose. If he got an audience, he would discuss the merits of his work—try to garner patronage—not chat about the benefits of a drink which instilled such debate among the masses.

He, shrugged, letting the Moor down gently. "The point is moot—for my work is not acclaimed enough to reach the attention of the pope."

The Moor smiled. "And if it were?"

Battista could not disappoint him. "Then I would sing its praises to Pope Clement."

"Then I can do nothing less than help you," the Moor said.

At last, after weeks of waiting, Battista was led into the small chamber Pope Clement used for audiences. Painting after painting filled the dark, paneled walls—beautiful, religious art of the holy family and the death of Christ and more. Battista recognized several paintings by DaVinci and Raphael—prominently placed—and dozens more by artists he couldn't name, their paintings hung higher, or lower, hidden in the shadows cast by the oil lamps.

Compared to the immenseness of the Vatican, this room was small, able to hold only a dozen or so comfortably. Pope Clement sat on a throne, a high-backed and ornately carved wooden chair, the same dark-stained color as the room's paneling. He looked like a bird in a tree—a cardinal—his papal robes bright red against the dark wood, the lamplight reflecting off the bejeweled silver pectoral cross resting on his chest. His beard was nearly as silver.

Pope Clement curled a hand, beckoning Battista closer.

Suddenly nervous, Battista suppressed a laugh bubbling up in his throat, and hoped not to embarrass himself. He alone had the pope's attention! He could have danced a jig, knowing what an opportunity this was.

Instead, he moved to the pope on shaking legs, and with more decorum than he felt, he knelt and kissed Pope Clement's ring, then received a blessing.

"If I may, Your Holiness," Battista rose and lifted his bag and small coffee pot to show Pope Clement, "I would like to prepare for you a cup of coffee before we speak. "

Pope Clement smiled, beckoning Battista closer. He spoke very softly. "You may pour me some coffee. You know, I have been curious about this drink which my advisors tell me it is a product of the devil, and which has the faithful asking if they may enjoy it on fasting days."

Battista smiled at the confidence and prepared the coffee just as the Moor had taught him, starting with cold water he had brought from the stream at Gianicolo Hill and using the small fireplace in the Pope's receiving room to heat the water.

"I must do more than simply pour it, your Holiness. I must brew it." Battista placed the copper pot of clear water into the hearth, close enough to the flames to become hot, but not near enough to boil. He pulled out two plain cups, wishing he'd spent money on something finer to serve the Pope. *Why hadn't the Moor given him something better to work with?*

"How is it made?" Pope Clement asked.

Battista showed him the fine, dark granules. "We measure these finely ground pieces of the roasted coffee bean, toss them in the pot after the water heats, and wait for them to settle—"

"You stir and then drink?" Clement asked, leaning forward to watch Battista make the coffee.

Battista shook his head and pulled out a small cloth sack. "Stirring may cause it to bitter. The grounds must sink." He touched the sack. "Then we'll add a bit of sugar, let it heat some more, and then stir, allowing a dark foam to rise to the surface of the brew. "

"It has a marvelous aroma," Clement said, sniffing the air. "I can almost taste in now."

Battista nodded, agreeing completely, and prepared the drink as he spoke, finally pouring the thick, dark liquid into one of the small cups, and handed it to the pope.

Pope Clement raised the cup to his nose, breathed in the steaming tendrils rising from the surface of the liquid, and took a tiny sip. He smiled, sipped again, and then sipped a third time. He gestured for Battista to join him in the chair to his right. "This devil's drink is so delicious…" Pope Clement smiled. "… that we should cheat the devil by baptizing it."

"I agree!" Battista gushed, lifting his own cup from the small table, and walking to the offered chair, sat beside the Pope. He sipped his coffee, savoring the strong, sweet flavor on his tongue. And when he judged enough time had passed for the Pope to enjoy his drink, Battista ventured to change the subject to his poetry. "Again, your Holiness, I would like to say, I am honored to be here today." He gave the Pope a small bow from the waist. "I thank you for your recognition of my work—"

The door cracked open and the Pope's assistant walked in, crossing quickly to Pope Clement and whispered in his ear. The pope listened and nodded, listened more and nodded again, and turned to Battista. He offered his ring for a kiss. "That's all we have time for today, I'm afraid. I thank you for the coffee."

"But my poetry—" Battista stood as the Pope rose from his throne.

"Regretfully, we have no more time to talk," said the Pope. He settled his empty cup on a small table.

The meeting was over.

Disconsolate, Battista gathered his things and departed.

The Moor waited for Battista on the bench beneath Tasso's oak. He drank from a cup of coffee and offered Battista one from the flask once the poet sat.

"Did the pope enjoy his coffee?" The Moor asked, leaning back against the bench, crossing one leg over the other and resting the flask in the crook of his bent knee.

"He did." Battista sipped from the coffee, the dark foam staining his upper lip, the heat warming his insides, wondering where it had all gone wrong. "Pope Clement liked it enough to joke about baptizing it and stealing it away from the devil."

The Moor chuckled. "There was never any need for that." He poured himself another cup from the flask. "And your verse—were you able to discuss it?"

Shaking his head, Battista gave the Moor a mournful look. "There was no time once we discussed the coffee."

"That's too bad," said the Moor, nodding, his own eyes mirroring Battista's sad ones. He took the last drink from his cup and laid it on the bench. Then, he stood, closed the flask, and tucked it into his brocade vest and patted it. "I must be gone."

Battista rose, too, setting his cup next to the Moor's. "So soon?" He would have enjoyed some company, someone to share his burdens with.

"My work here is done." He held out a hand to Battista.

Battista shook the Moor's hand, remembering the tail, which was nowhere in sight. Again, the odor of sulfur reached his nose.

The Moor took his leave, and Battista watched him trod down the hill until the steep angle hid him from view. Then he sat, and reached for his coffee.

But both cups were gone.

What historical period did you choose and what attracted you to it?

I chose the time period of 16th century Italy for the *Devil's Brew*. I'd seen a 1960s painting by artist Peter Blume, *Tasso's Oak,* which spurred the idea. Italy has always fascinated me, and I've spent some time there, so I did some research on the poet Tasso. Poor Tasso waited for the Pope to recognize his genius, and died—still waiting—under the oak that bears his name. I found the story fascinating and wondered what would have happened if Tasso would have actually gotten his audience with the Pope.

What did you change and what do you see the fallout from it to be?

In my story, the poet actually gets his audience with the Pope; it does not go as expected—as these things usually do.

What texts were crucial to your research?

I first saw Blume's painting in an old magazine, *Horizon Magazine,* which I pulled off a shelf in a vacation cottage. The article was fascinating. Afterward, I did some internet research to finalize details about the Pope and Tasso's poetry.

What is a good introduction to this period?

A good introduction to the time might be Niccolò Machiavelli's *The Prince*, which many people are already familiar with. Martin Luther's Bible appeared in the same time frame, as did *Institutes of the Christian Religion* by John Calvin. In fact, many, many religious texts were published in this time period (including *The Lamentations of a Sinner* by Queen Catherine Parr—the widow of Henry the VIII—and the first woman to publish in English under her own name.) For something lighter, one might try Nicolaus Copernicus' *On the Revolution of the Heavenly Spheres*, or, Francis Bacon's *Essays*.

circa 1680

POISON HEART
Russell Hemmell

"Do you know the name of this woman?" The policeman asks, pointing an accusatory finger at the lady in black in front of me.

"No."

"How does she know yours, then?"

"She came searching for that plant." I shrug. "Yes, the one you're holding right now."

He drops the sachet with a grunt. "Are you aware she's connected to a dangerous divineresse, known to have poisoned many people?"

I look at the two with tranquillity. Police don't scare me; in their eyes, I'm just one of the thousand motherless children of Paris stealing and begging for the Gran Consroe. "So what?" I reply, spitefully. "I just gave her what she wanted."

They appraise me for a moment, and the higher in rank is the first to speak. "Let the boy go. He doesn't know shit."

The other seems more doubtful. "Let's take him to De La Reynie. We caught him with evidence of a crime, after all."

"Yes, water hemlock." His colleague shakes his head. "If we had to apprehend all kids for what they trade or steal, the Chatelet would soon run out of space."

"That's a poisonous component-"

"Found pretty much everywhere if you know where to look for it." He laughs. "These brats...they'd sell their own mothers for money. You." He glares at me. "Out of my sight. If I catch you again with the hemlock-"

I bow and touch his hands with ostentatious gratitude. "Thank you, Sir."

I turn on my heels and I walk intentionally into the other guard. He yells whilst I flash an apology and leave Rue de la Lune in a hurry, not without having unburdened him from a couple of ecus.

"Where've you been, you useless beggar?" My handler barks with his habitual good manners when I reach the Court of Miracles.

As soon as he sees the gold, however, he shuts up and waves his hand to dismiss me. I go to the tavern next door. They're not supposed to allow me in, but the owner's son is my friend, and now, squatting on the kitchen's floor, I treat myself to beer and mutton. All considered, the Court of Miracles ain't a bad place, at least until I can live without giving the impression I've anything to hide. So far I managed, but dangers are everywhere, and it's not the police I'm talking about, but churches, priests and monks. They'd burn me at the stake, like my mother years ago. She was a witch, they said, and a heretic, and the only thing to do with witches and heretics is a cheerful bûcher in Place de Greve. France's an unsafe place now, and lots of people end that way. So many women accused of consorting with the Devil, when they just tried to make a living. Not my case, though. My mother was a real sorciere, and so am I. The only difference is that I look like a 10-year-old boy instead of the 13-year-old girl I am, and that suits me fine.

I look at the coin. I'm good at it, but stealing is not what I do best. I'm a healer, something that comes from my mother's side, from that ancient, hidden species of women my family line from mother's side belongs to. A species about which I don't know a lot, including the puzzling question why we look like normal people—elfin look, webbed feet, and tangled, messy red hair nonetheless. Mother never told me anything, maintaining that ignorance would've been my best protection. I'm not sure about that: it left me without a past and with a future I can't foresee, even though at times I get a glimpse of the others' future, a gift I don't like and I don't control anyway. About this morning's encounter with the police, I had no foresight of any kind.

The lady in black came to the Court of Miracles a few nights ago, asking for water hemlock. Somebody told her I prepare potions for the sick, and she assumed, not so unreasonably, that whoever's able to heal is able to kill. She offered a lot of money, but I couldn't avoid thinking that my mother would've never accepted to harm an innocent. She was maybe consorting with the Devil as they said—I still wonder about that; I've only seen her with humans for what I can remember—but she was a gentle soul. Me, I'm just one of the orphans of Paris, dirty, nasty, and soulless, so I don't really care, do I?

Still, I eventually decided to give her something that could pass for hemlock but was innocuous—water parsnip. The lady couldn't poison anybody with that more than she could with an onion soup. But it looked suspiciously like the poisonous plant she was after, and, unfortunately for her, the police believed it, too. Feigning ignorance was the safest of the options, and the fact I'm now eating up to my gourd while she's at Vincennes proves me right. The thought of that woman doesn't leave my mind, however. How is she now—is she in troubles because of me?

I walk back to my dwelling, and, before I lie down to my bench, I have a quick, harrowing vision of the woman: tied up, blindfolded, and burning at the stake. I fall into agitated dreams.

I'm on my way to Les Halles after a restless night. And as I cross the Court of Miracles' invisible but effective borders, a hand sizes my shirt.

"Leave me. Now," I growl, trying to kick my captor's ankles.

"Can't, kid," he says, in a gentle but unapologetic voice. He drags me to a church, where he forces me to sit on a wooden bench. "Be quiet and listen."

"Are you police?"

"No."

"Liar," I glare. "I recognise the King's men when I see one. I don't speak with them, or with their spies."

"I'm no spy either."

"Who are you then?" I appraise him. He's young, handsome, with piercing eyes. Educated and rich, from the way he dresses and talks.

"A judge—interested in the crime the police's persecuting right now." He sits in front of me but keeping at some distance. "You know well what they're after."

"Poison?"

"And witchcraft, too."

I'm sure my cheeks get paler when he pronounces that word. I bite my lips.

"You were there when Madame Brinvilliers was burnt at the stake," he says, quietly.

"Like many others."

"But you had a good reason. You're Mathilde's daughter, after all," he continues.

I ain't sure what to say to that. "Did you know her?"

"No. I knew your father."

"Who, the Devil?"

The young man laughs. "They call Jesuits in a lot of ways, and Christian Lorrain with all sort of names, but that's original indeed."

"The hell with him," I sneer. "He left my mother to die and me alone."

"No, kid. He was executed, allegedly for conspiring with the Huguenots."

A Jesuit with the Protestants? These people lack logic.

He seems to read my mind. "It doesn't matter what I personally believe. After his death, nobody could save your mother. You've been lucky they let you go."

"Why are you telling me all this? You're not here to protect me."

"Unlikely: judges aren't a generous kind." His tone is calm and collected when he speaks. "And you don't need protection."

At least I can't say he's a hypocrite. "So why are you after me?"

"I'm not after you. But I do need your help."

"My help? For what?" I throw a brief glimpse around, but the church looks deserted.

"The Affair of Poison now raging in Paris."

"I don't see how I can possibly be of any help. Or why I should get involved in the first place."

"Because you already are," he says. "I've seen you yesterday."

This conversation is taking a turn I don't like. I squirm uncomfortably on the wooden bench. "I haven't given that lady anything dangerous."

"I know." He smiles. "I'll tell you a story. Lady's name is Anne, and she's in business with a woman called Catherine Deshayes. Otherwise called La Voisin."

"Haven't heard of her."

"You will, together with the whole city. She's been arrested for poisoning and witchcraft and soon to be condemned—not the first to be burnt at the stake and certainly not the last. Your Anne's going to follow, with many others of all ages and conditions. Like your mother."

"Wait a minute." I raise my hands. "My mother never poisoned anybody."

"Your mother was in the wrong place at the wrong time, as they're now."

"I don't–"

"There's a girl, called Marguerite. She's La Voisin's daughter, and she knows everything about her mother's crimes," he says. "She's innocent, but she has witnessed facts that can shake France to its roots. Marguerite has not enough courage to go forward and speak, but she won't stay silent either if interrogated. She told me she can't live with this remorse on her conscience and asked me to denounce her to the authorities."

There's clearly something I'm missing here. "So what do you need me for?"

"To give Marguerite away. That is, exchanging her against the freedom of some of the innocents imprisoned in Vincennes."

I'm no longer confused. I'm at loss for words, and he notices my bewilderment. "Some are languishing in jail, but there's no proof against them. You can manage to get them out of the hook."

"I thought you want them condemned."

The man bends toward me and I have a good look at his eyes. Pale, dark grey eyes, cold but not hostile. "No. Many of them are cheaters, fortune-tellers, at worst thieves, but not poisoners. They've never killed anybody, only got caught in games bigger than they can even imagine. They were stupid, sure, but this is not a crime."

"There's more than that."

"Obviously. I told you I'm not generous. I have a personal interest in closing this case as soon as possible. I'm just giving you some good reasons why you should help me."

"You could denounce her," I object.

"My political allegiances will make it look like a set-up, and Marguerite's story won't be believed. Not when they hear what she's going to tell. Regarding me-" he adds, pre-empting my next question. "I work with Colbert. The King's Minister." He looks at the altar in the middle of the church. "Colbert thinks this story has been going on too long and is a way of delivering political vendettas among nobles, not persecuting culprits. De La Reynie will have to draw the curtain, the sooner, the better."

"Why should I care? All these rich and powerful people… let them rot in hell." I glance at the altar, too, staring at the candles' flickering lights. What kind of religion is one that has an instrument of torture—a cross—as its symbol? I shiver, in spite of myself. "That won't get my mother back from the grave."

"No, It won't, and some of them deserve what they got," he says. "They might even be real poisoners, like Catherine

Trianon or Marie Bosse; but others are not. They're like you, only less fortunate."

Our eyes meet again, and I know he's telling the truth. I'm the first to blink. "What you want me to do, exactly?"

"Go and meet De La Reynie. Offer him definitive information and material witnesses about La Voisin's practices, and ask something in exchange: the freedom of a few prisoners. You'll give him a list of names."

"I don't have those name."

"Not yet." He reaches for his bag and hands me a leather folder. "They're all here, together with their latest depositions. I know you can read."

"Moving sheets?" I say, not without irony.

"Quite convenient in a trial about sensitive issues." He says, without missing a beat.

"The Chief of the Police might just throw me in jail. Have you thought about it?"

"It's a risk, yes. No matter how convincing the story can be, success will eventually reside in your own ability to persuade him," he replies. "But the offer's appealing, and the fact you ask something in return will make it more persuasive."

"Tell me something. Why, if this confession is so important, it will produce the opposite effect? You said it's going to shut down the investigation, which seems not what De La Reynie wants."

He taps on the folder's leather cover. "Because the identity of the culprits, and the enormity of their crimes, will eventually prove their safeguard. The King will put an end to it. De La Reynie will have no choice."

"So you're delivering him a poisoned gift."

"Appropriate, isn't it?" I see a glint of amusement on his face. "I'm giving him what he wants the most: a full confession and shocking details about this already complicated affair. Sometimes having our wishes granted's a curse, not a blessing—a thing he's going to discover."

A couple of people pass by on their way out of the church. His hands join in prayer, while I lower my head to avoid being stared at.

"You think too much of me," I say, without looking at him.

"I knew your father. And no matter which powers you might or might not have got from your mother, your real asset's your intelligence. Use it now. Use it for the ones who can't stand for themselves."

My eyes fill up with unexpected tears, and I have to make an effort to avoid crying. My fingers caress the folder, flipping through the documents. I realise I don't even know this man's name.

"I'm Gabriel."

Is he a Seer, too, maybe? Startling that he reads me so well. "Martin."

"That's a boy's name. It must be Martine." He smiles.

"Martin," I repeat. "I'll speak to de la Rayne. Maybe I'll succeed. But we won't talk again, whatever it happens."

"Tomorrow we're going to discuss operative details. After that, you'll be on your own. Whatever it happens."

He observes me with a pensive expression. "I can't say Christian and I were friends, but we respected each other and would've been on the same side in this circumstance." Gabriel stands up. "You have your father's ice-blue eyes, Martine, his strength and his logic. I hope they'll serve you well."

I open my mouth, but any reply making sense eludes me. I leave the church in a hurry.

The Chambre Ardente, that's the name of the special tribunal De La Reynie set up, has made since the beginning precise choices about this trial. No ordinary prison for the suspects, not even the Conciergerie where Madame de Brinvilliers, the first poisoner to be condemned, spent her detention. No—La Voisin and the others are securely held at Vincennes.

Did De La Reynie want to isolate them from the other criminals? I think about the line I've agreed with Gabriel while I head to the Arsenal, where La Bastille dominates the surroundings in all its dark majesty. My appointment with De La Reynie has been immediately granted, like Gabriel had predicted. I enter the room. It's sombre—suiting well the Chief of Police's notoriously severe mood.

I look at him, Nicolas De La Reynie. A man in his fifties, and from humble origins like my mother. We've something else in common: the year I was born he got his post here, coming directly from the good grace of Mr. Colbert, the very man that now is trying to stop him. Destiny works indeed in mysterious ways. The Chief of Police's known, and hated, by everybody in the Court of Miracles—but he's not stupid, and not a fanatic either. I know for a fact he defended and protected Protestants against persecution, and that's something you can get in serious troubles for, no matter how powerful you are.

"You said you had critical evidence regarding the Affair of Poisons, evidence that may change the course of this process." He looks at me, cold eyes on a tired face.

"Yes." Gabriel got me some suitable clothes, and now I look like one of the young men of Les Halles' shops, street-smart and far away from intrigues of all kind. But I'm scared nonetheless. I've taken a huge risk coming here; telling this fearsome man a subjective truth—how else I can define it—is not even the worst one.

"Speak then. What do we have overlooked?"

"Not what. Who."

I repeat what Gabriel has instructed me to say. The young lady called Marguerite, the confession, the horrible crimes still undiscovered. I don't omit anything, except her identity. "Many people you arrested have nothing to do with the murderers. They've just traded things like this." I take a tuft of water parsnip out of my pocket and leave it on the huge wooden desk that stands between us.

He looks at the herbs with attention. "How can you tell?"

"I know names."

"So you're announcing yourself as an accomplice."

"Yes. But not of murder, only of cheating," I say. "Everybody in Paris knows about this frenzy, and a lot of beggars in the Court of Miracles have tried to take advantages of these rich, stupid women willing to pay so much money for this fake stuff."

"People died for real."

"Not because of this plant." I eat the tuft in front of him. "It can easily pass for hemlock, but it's not."

"Tell me those names, boy." He says, after a moment.

I produce the list I've put together in the last two days. Gabriel has left me precise notes about the prisoners and what they're accused of, even though he made clear that the call between who to save and who to let die would've been mine. I'm aware he doesn't care about any of them, but he didn't lie to me: some of them are indeed poor people, and they're the ones I'm going to rescue. "They're here awaiting an unjust trial."

He squints his eyes. "Not unjust. They still tried to kill people."

"With what I've given them they couldn't kill their cat."

"Some have been accused of murdering children and performing black masses."

"Have you actually found bones in their houses?" I say. "Maybe others in this process have—but not them."

"They've declared to have summoned the Devil, too," he says, slowly.

I try not to show my contempt. "You wouldn't believe the Devil's going to be lured with such cheap tricks, would you? Provided He exists."

"Don't be blasphemous. If you believe in God, you believe in the Devil."

I don't need to be a Seer to know I'd better abandon this dangerous ground. "But you don't believe this is witchcraft more than I do."

"You're right, I don't." Nicolas looks at me, an earnest look into his eyes. "But I do believe in conspiracies against my King."

"This is why I'm here. You should concentrate on the real culprits." I point at the list. "Let these people go, Monsieur Le Chef de la Police. I'll give you what you're after: the enemies of our King, the ones that conspired against him. That young lady's willing to talk, and she'll tell you everything about La Voisin and her whole network."

I see what he's evaluating now whether he can believe me and whether he should arrest and torture me to get that name anyway. I feel his indecision, and for some timeless instants I hold my breath. Like everything in life, the choice between survival and death, safety and damnation, is a matter of a few instants. He takes the list from the table.

"Deal. Deliver me that woman, and I'll let you have the ones against whom no circumstantial evidence has emerged so far. From what I can see—" I watch his eyes scanning quickly the dozens of names I've put in, "—is one-third of them. The children of a destitute city, who have to survive in any way, not always rightful." He doesn't add "like us" but I know what's thinking. I nod in silence.

He stands up, leaving the list on his desk.

"One-third, you said...what about the others? Are they already burnt meat?"

"No. But they're going to pay for their involvement in this sordid business."

"They're still innocent, only comparatively wealthier." The meeting is coming to its end. I collect my stuff. "They're no worse than the rest, stupid and ignorant just the same."

"They are, yes." He looks at me, with a hard stare. "But they've no excuses for their ignorance."

Time has passed since I've been at the Arsenal.

I still think about that conversation with De La Reynie every time I walk past by Saint-Antoine, which it doesn't happen that often. I tend to avoid that place, the way I'd love to forget about the Affair of Poisons altogether.

But I cannot—nor can Paris.

It is July, and heat torments the city, with the lack of water, flies, and even more filth on the lurid streets. But there's something to entertain Parisians today, and it's the execution of Anne Poligny, the one I handed water parsnip to, for murder and witchcraft.

"They're almost done with the pyre," a little boy beside me shouts. "It's going to begin soon. Look."

I look.

Anne has been unlucky; as Gabriel previewed, the Chambre Ardente and the whole investigation had been shut down soon after Marguerite started talking, but I've been unable to regain her freedom in my trade of lost souls with the Chief of the Police. Maybe this is why I'm Place de Greve now, like five years ago.

My feet hurt for the long wait—preparing a bûcher is a laborious process—and I'm thirsty, but I force myself to stay put. I owe this to her.

The boy's right: the pyre is ready, with hay and twigs and combustibles heaped up around the massive stake at the centre of the stage. I can smell the oil stench from where I stand.

A high-pitched sound rises from behind my shoulders.

"The Witch is here," the crowd screams, parting to let the procession in with the prisoner in tow.

Here is she, indeed, blindfolded the way I've seen her in my vision, and with a dress in tatters, wriggling in fear while they literally drag her toward the execution ground.

Anne Poligny won't be the last one I'll have to watch die, this I know. Others will follow.

It's ironic—people in Paris get condemned for reading the future, a capability they only feign to have. Somebody like me, who can do it for real, walks free. I had more visions since I've written that list for De La Reynie. Scary ones, of people I don't even know—as the young girl that's now tottering around like a newborn lamb a few metres from me. Her name is Marie-Anne de La Ville, and rosy cheeks and blue eyes won't save her one day from this same ghastly death.

"Death to the Poisoners," the people around me cheer.

The executioners have secured Anne's waist and wrists to the iron clamps fastened to the stake and they've lightened up the torches, while the monk approached to offer her the last rites.

I flinch and try instead to think about the rest, the ones I was able to save. Surprisingly or not, De La Reynie has maintained his word and freed a few people off my list. His estimates were right and about 60 people were able to walk out free from the Arsenal.

I've often wondered why he accepted my proposal when he could've arrested me: torturing me for half a day would've made the job. I've never found a satisfactory explanation. I've concluded that it was because, perhaps, he was tired as well to have the destitute children of Paris paying the price when the noble and the powerful were the ones he was against. If that's correct, I have only given him a good excuse for something he would have liked to do anyway. Even under this aspect, Gabriel seemed to have read him well.

"I'd love to see all La Voisin's accomplices burning at the stake," a man nearby says. "Not just the ones who got caught."

"They probably will," I reply, incapable of taking my eyes away from Anne. The wood ignites and she coughs, and screams, and cries among the flames creeping up her gown.

"Nah. The Tribunal must've been scared about what she might say. So they didn't torture her and preferred executing the damn witch straight away."

He's police, I reckon. He knows details and he's dressed better than the others.

"And the others? They've not even been judged," he continues, spitting on the ground. "They've been imprisoned by a lettre of cachet, and sealed away together with their depositions."

And left to die in a forgotten prison, I complete mentally. I'm not sure that's better. "Are you surprised? Madame de Montespan was implicated, too, I've heard," I offer.

"The worst-kept secret in Paris," he sneers. "Many of the King's inner court were involved, too. And Montespan, well… she dealt in black masses and human sacrifices. In one of them, a renegade priest puts an infant on her naked body before slashing the poor baby's neck to summon the Devil."

"No wonder the King has shut everything down, then."

I close my eyes under a cold, sudden gust of wind that touches my face like the caress of ghost and in a moment I see her, Marguerite. After her confession, they've sent her far away, in a place called Belle-Il-en-Mer, a sort of prison without walls in an island off the coast of Brittany.

And there she is now, walking by the sea, in solitude, her light dress moved by the marine breeze, a tormented soul and hair cut down in a nun-like fashion. She has been sentenced to observe silence, but that's something that suits her just fine. La Voisin's daughter has told the world all she needed to, and she has no appetite for shallow talks. I could hold myself responsible for her exile, but I know, somehow, this unjust punishment has been more welcomed than dreaded. I see her smiling.

The jarring yells of the crowd bring me back.

I sense somebody's looking at me, and I turn my head. Gabriel is there, just a few meters away. Our stares dance together for a long moment, and this time I don't blink. He bows his head and leaves, without saying a word.

Anne is not screaming any longer. They've refused to strangle her beforehand—no mercy for the poisoners—but the smoke has made the deed, granting her a swift death before the flames could gobble up her body. It is the crowd that captures my eyes now. They seem transfixed, bewitched by what looks more a theatrical performance than a real execution.

And me...for once, I'm not scared of what I am, not any longer. Because now I know I come from a million-year-old species that has always existed, in a subdued way, walking on the ground alongside the humans and never sharing the planet with them. Fearful and feared, we had to hide and slither, going out at night to avoid being chased during the day, and my mother paid with her life the refusal of her kind and the love for a human.

I've finally started understanding why, after having resented her for years. It would've been so easy to follow Gabriel and wait by his side to become an adult. So tempting. I can't deny I felt this urge, and I can forgive my mother for having given in. But I won't make her same mistake. I will rather go and search for my kind, wherever it is now hidden. I will find out who I am. And maybe one day I'll be back here, to him or to whatever remains of this city.

The ceremony is over, and the majority of people have left Place de Greve. Not everybody, though: some of them linger on, exchanging stares, whispering comments.

I approach the pyre and go down on my knees, feigning a prayer. I've seen the face of my mother in this dying lady I've contributed to murder, and for a while I was there again, blind with rage and seething for vengeance against a fanatic humanity incapable of handling diversity.

Now even that hatred is gone.

I brush the still warm cinders, sizzling remains of the same fire that consumed by mother's flesh, and I'm no longer sure the Devil doesn't exist. But he's not what these people fear, or desire. Le Diable lives in the darkest recesses of their mind, ready to stir up and insinuate himself into their greedy instincts; and he poisons human hearts whenever their reason sleeps, and their compassion fades.

A heavy cloak on my shoulders, a velvet hat on my head, my hands grip the folder with the defendants' names, while I walk on the road that will take me away from Paris—towards an unknown world full of wonders and a future of more tolerance. I'm hopeful and ready.

What historical period did you choose and what attracted you to it?
This is France of mid-1600s and the famous Affair of Poisons. How can I not be attracted?

What did you change and what do you see the fallout from it to be?
I changed very little. Apart from Martine, who is a Seer and half-human, and Gabriel, all the others are historical characters and everything in the story happened for real, including La Voisin's daughter and her fate. The lesson is about fanaticism and its risks.

What texts were crucial to your research?
I have used a few historical sources (I am a bilingual French speaker, and that helped when researching this period):

Anne Somerset (2003) *The Affair of the Poisons: Murder, Infanticide, and Satanism at the Court of Louis XIV,* London: St. Martin's Press

Lynn Wood Mollenauer (2007) *Strange Revelations: Magic, Poison, and Sacrilege in Louis XIV's France,* University Park: Pennsylvania State University Press. 2007.

Éric Le Nabour (1990) *La Reynie: Le policier de Louis XIV,* Paris: Perrin

François Ravaisson, *Archives de la Bastille, Paris, 1866–1884, Volumes IV, V, VI, VII*

What is a good introduction to this period?
There are a lot of excellent resources on the web about 1600s France. I would also suggest: Colin Jones, 2006, *Paris: The Biography of a City,* London: Penguin

circa 1850

MOTHER OF SANDS
Stewart C. Baker

Smilšu māte, mother of sands—how I wish I had never heard that name, that I had never learned what waits on the far shore of that river we cross upon dying. But I have, and I did, and I must share what I witnessed with you, my closest friends.

It began last September, at the end of that hot, dry summer. I received a letter from the Countess of —, whom I had known as a girl through my mother, who had been her lady's maid. Although as children we had often played together, I had not heard from her in fifteen years, and was much amazed that she remembered me—let alone that she had thought to send me a letter.

My dearest Clara, the letter began, and went on at some length about the rigours of life amidst the landed gentry which I, in my rented room in gloomy Stepney, cared little to read. Towards the end, though, was a section that riveted my eyes:

In short, my dearest Clara, I find myself quite bereft of the friendship we shared in our youth, and should like nothing more than to renew it. It would grant my fondest hope should you accompany me to my native Riga to visit my mother, who has taken ill.

The letter was signed with my old friend's given name of Ilze. At this I laughed and shook my head, quite certain that I was the recipient of a passing aristocratic fancy, and nothing more.

So it was that I set the affair from my mind and went back to my writing.

The days wound on until a full month passed and I was surprised by a knocking at my door. I opened it, steeling myself to be set upon by some creditor or unhappy patron, and met instead with Ilze's smiling face.

"You did not return my letter," she admonished, "but it does not matter. I have everything prepared."

I sputtered my protests—I had work still to do as my creditors would never let me rest—but they fell on deaf ears. Ilze spirited me down the stairs to a waiting carriage, where she plied me with stories of her life. Such was her enthusiasm that I could not so much as speak, let alone request that she return me to my home. Truth be told, I did not try too hard, for while I still felt my old friend would discard me as soon as she grew bored, I had resolved to enjoy the unexpected respite from my worries for as long as it lasted.

We passed the day in a pleasant enough fashion, and stopped for the evening in the seaside town of Southend, where Ilze insisted on a shared room at a common inn. I considered it odd that we had not departed by boat from London, and that she had no servants with her; her insistence on sharing a room was doubly strange. But I did not speak of it: who was I to question the Countess of —?

It was here that the first strange event of our journey occurred. That evening as the sun set, Ilze suddenly paled and rushed me from the inn's dining hall to the room we were to share. I asked what was wrong, but she would say only Smilšu māte—the words croaked out from between her lips like a curse and a prayer all at once.

In our quarters, she walked all around with a candle, thrusting it here and there until the shadows danced with movement. After some minutes of this, she placed the candle on the sill, locked the door, and collapsed into bed, sobbing.

I tried to get some sensible response from her, but it was futile. Growing weary myself, I at last reached for the candle myself and blew it out, thinking to sleep. But just as the light guttered away into night's inky blackness, I saw as clear as day a woman standing over my companion, her eyes pooled shadows in her pinched, drawn face.

My heart hammered in my ears; I scarcely dared breathe, so fearful was I. At length, enough moonlight filtered through the window for me to see the woman was gone. Nonetheless I could not calm myself, and lay wakeful all through the long night, with only Ilze's hiccoughing sobs to distract me.

Though Ilze and I did not speak of it, the first thing we did that morning was search our quarters thoroughly. We found no sign of the woman, only a small heap of dull, brownish-grey sand. Ilze quaked when she saw this, and quickly scattered it about, muttering something in her native tongue, though she would not say why or what.

"It is bad luck to speak of such things," she told me.

"Smilšu māte?" I asked. "Who is she? What does it mean?"

But Ilze only shook her head, and would say no more.

The rest of our trip passed slowly but uneventfully, and I need spend no time here in recounting it. We went by ship to Amsterdam, and from that squat, bustling port travelled again by carriage. Neither in our cabin nor in any of the inns where we stayed did I again see the woman, though on occasion we found a small heap of sand, which Ilze dealt with in the manner of the first.

We arrived in Riga, the heart of old Livonia, on the first day of November, more than month after setting out. You who have never visited that distant place will know nothing of its cobbled streets. It will mean nothing to you if I speak of the way the stately Daugava flows past the city's many spires, its frigid waters surprisingly strong.

Ilze's mother lived in a narrow three story house painted in a delicate green. Huddled amidst more expansive buildings, it seemed to cling to the edge of the cobblestones, afraid of losing its place. Ilze clapped at the door and entered without waiting for a response, and I followed her reluctantly, for the building birthed in me a nameless unease.

Inside, the walls pressed in on me. They reminded me of our worries. If Ilze felt anything of what I did, however, she did not show it; indeed, compared to the pale, nervous woman I had known on our journey, here in the rooms of her earliest moments she was a different person entire. She strode from room to room on the ground floor, calling out in her native language, and did not seem to mind when there was no response.

"Mama must be out," she said with a smile. "Come; I shall show you the sights of the town."

But no sooner had we set out that her face took on its familiar melancholy cast. She became listless, and offered no commentary as we strolled from sight to sight, across age-worn bridges and along the banks of the Daugava. I saw a pleasure steamer plying the waters, festooned with flags and filled with travelers. Marveling at its existence in this antique place, I mentioned that I should like to try it. But, as ever, Ilze would not be drawn out, and I heard no word from her until we returned to her mother's home with the sun pinking the sky.

A light was on in the ground floor window, and my earlier unease returned. I found myself looking for sand as Ilze led me inside, and my heart's blood thrummed in my ears as it had that night when I saw the shadow-pool woman.

My fears proved unfounded. Reclining in a chaise lounge was a woman I had never seen before, but who was clearly Ilze's mother: she had the same rich brown hair, the same slightly square face, and the set of her eyes somehow spoke to me, pulling me along despite myself.

"You are late," she said, in slightly accented English. "I had started to fear you would not arrive."

"Oh, mother," Ilze said, reproachful. "Of course I had to come when I heard you were sick."

"Ha! A year ago and more I sent that letter. A strange form of concern you show me, daughter, when you tarry for so long, and bring an uninvited guest when at last you arrive."

Even behind Ilze, I could see her skin flush. "I had pressing business to attend to," she said. "After you sold me to the Count in marriage, my life has not been my own. And it is so remote here that travel alone is—"

"Remote! You speak this way the land where you were born? I should never have sent you to England, no matter the prize. You—"

Ilze snapped out in her native tongue, and her mother responded in kind. Their voices grew louder as they argued, and not wanting to intrude further than I already had, I stepped into the next room, where tables were laid out with an astounding feast. There were rolls, cheese, and butter by the bowlful; fine cuts of roast and fowl; and delicacies I could not name. Balls of dough adorned with hemp seed filled a plate next to pastries overflowing with a thick, white cream.

Where had it all come from, I wondered. Who was it for? I had seen no servants in the house, nor any other guests. At a loss for what I might do to pass the time, I popped a pastry into my mouth. Almond paste in the cream, I thought, or something like it—sweet almost to bitterness. Still, I had not eaten in some time and it was good enough. I took another.

At length the shouting in the next room subsided, and Ilze and her mother entered, their arms entwined for all the world as though they had not just been engaged in a fight of the most intimate sort.

"Your pardon, Clara, dearest," Ilze said to me, breaking away from her mother. "In this part of the world we believe it better to air out our emotions."

"It is true," her mother said, as she ushered me to one of the chairs, "no matter what part of the world you find yourself in. You English would be more agreeable did you not bottle up your feelings so. Now sit, and we will show you another of our customs: the feast of the dead."

"All this is for the dead?" The pastries in my stomach heavy as rocks.

Ilze laughed. "Of course not. But it is tradition to give them the first morsel, and the first draught of mead."

"Especially tonight," her mother added, "for on the night after Simjudas, the dead can return to the living, to take back for those who have offended them." And with a light, tinkling laughter, she poured a splash of alcohol into the fireplace, following it with one of the dough balls.

My tongue burned; I only hoped the colour did not spread to my cheeks. Neither Ilze nor her mother seemed to notice. Each piled her plate high with food and filled her cup with mead. Reluctantly, I did the same, although I supposed there was no harm in my inadvertent breaking of their pagan custom so long as they did not know it.

We ate in an uncomfortable silence for a time, until, casting around for some topic of conversation, I said to Ilze's mother: "I am glad to see, Mrs. —, that you have at least regained your health."

The older woman's eyes darkened, and I cursed myself. Why had I brought up the very thing which had caused her and Ilze to erupt earlier?

But I had no need for concern, it seemed; after a moment, the older woman smiled and said, "I will tell you how it came about."

And with that she launched into a story that I myself would not believe, were it not for what happened after.

Last year (Ilze's mother said), I caught a coughing sickness that would not leave me. The doctors could not cure me, and the prayers of a local priest rumoured to perform miracles failed as well. On the 29th of September, I began to cough blood. ("The day is Saint Michael's," Ilze whispered, "and the start of the month of the dead.")

Despairing, I walked to the shores of the Daugava, certain that I had not long in this life. As I crossed one of the river's bridges, a cold wind overtook me and I fell into a coughing fit so violent that my knees went weak. When I recovered, so much black, clotted blood covered my handkerchief that I resolved to end my life there and then. I leapt into the river, which drew me down into its cold, smothering embrace.

I awoke on a shore I had never before seen: in place of the city were trees of oak and linden, flanked in the distance by rolling hills of a sandy, yellow-grey soil. I was bone wet and shivering, and next to me stood a woman with eyes the colour of shadow.

"You have forsaken the traditions," she said to me. "You sent your only daughter to an uncaring land, and your ancestors go hungry each year. That is why you suffer."

Her voice was like grit: fine and sharp and hard, impossible to shake free.

"What should I do then, Mother," I asked, shivering from more than damp—for I knew then who she was, and where I had found myself. "How can I gain your forgiveness?"

"Bring her back," she said. "I will take care of the rest."

With that she was gone, and I was alone. I staggered to my feet and walked upstream, thinking to return to Riga. When at last I came upon a town, however, it was not my home, but a clump of simple dwellings surrounded by a wall of stakes as thick as trees.

The town's people seemed unable to hear me, and would not meet my eyes. I returned to the river, to gaze on its tranquil waters...

At this, Ilze's mother stopped talking, lost, it seemed, in reminiscence. Ilze, who had grown progressively paler throughout the recounting, gave no sign of talking. My own throat being dry as parchment, I took a swallow of mead and spoke.

"What then?"

Ilze's mother looked at me and smiled, but not pleasantly. Her face melted away, replaced by that of the woman I had seen over Ilze's bed that first night of our journey.

"Why, then, of course," she said, "she died." Her voice was just as Ilze's mother had described it.

She stood in one fluid motion; the candles guttered out, and the dark swarmed in with an inhuman shriek.

The rest of that night is a blur, all shadow and terror and ash. When I woke in the morning I found I had fallen asleep in a chair in the banquet room, and Ilze as well. The tables were empty save a patina of dust, and, search as we might, the two of us could find no evidence whatsoever that anyone lived in the house. All we found was a heap of yellow-grey sand in the front waiting room, where Ilze's mother had greeted us.

We passed some time huddled together, unsure and uncertain. I was of the opinion that the night's events had been hallucination, brought on perhaps by the fatigue of our journey, or by some ailment we had gathered to ourselves along the way. Ilze, contrarily, believed that we had seen her mother's ghost—that all she had spoken was true, and that Smilšu māte, the mother of sands, had granted her passage on the night of the feast so she might visit her absent daughter and (this in a darkening tone) take her to that other land by force.

"At least, then," I said, "you escaped the last. For you are here with me, alive."

Ilze only shook her head, and sank once more into gloom.

"Come," I said, "and I will show us both the truth of life." For I myself felt a need to be among people.

Ilze protested, but not with any heart, as I dragged her to the offices of the steamer I had seen the day before. Looking back, I cannot recall what moved me to think that a visit to the river—whence her mother claimed to have visited the other side of death—would take Ilze's mind off the previous night's occurrence. Perhaps it was the steamer itself, the only thing in that city which looked to the future instead of the past. Perhaps some stronger, stranger power was at work.

Whatever the reason, we had no trouble booking passage on the afternoon's cruise, and in short order were aboard the little ship's deck. The steamer was just as I had imagined it: a modern marvel, bursting with the energy of a new era, fueled by the powers of men turned to gods. Gliding past the banks of that provincial land suffused me with optimistic health, but all Ilze cared to do was stand and look into the waters of the river. I am afraid I must tell you I left her there, determined that I, at least, would find pleasure in the day's outing.

But we had been out barely half an hour when the boat began to shudder, and the deck pitched to one side with a crack and roaring boom. A mid-channel collision, I thought, or a fault in the hull. There was another jolt, the air filled with screams, and then the water hit me with a slap of icy cold.

As I sputtered, the truth came to me: it was Smilšu māte, come to claim her own. No sooner had I thought this than the power faded from my limbs and I resigned myself to death, but just before blackness took me, a surge of strength burst through in my limbs; a sudden passion rose in my heart. I would not die here, I resolved—not today! I broke the surface of the water and pushed to the river's edge with surprising ease, shivering in my thin traveling clothes. There was no sign of the steamer, the river's surface crowded with boats and men and ropes—a rescue, I thought, but too late, too late for poor Ilze and the rest.

I watched until evening, cold though I was. Hoping they would stumble across some miraculous survivor—that they would pull my old friend from the water still pink and full of breath, like me.

They found no one. As the rescuers returned to the shore, I asked what had happened, but none answered, lost perhaps in melancholy thoughts of their own. And though I waited by that shore until the moon came full in the sky, I never again saw any sign of Ilze.

Shuddering to think that I had nearly shared her fate, and eschewing any thoughts of Smilšu māte, or of the dead woman who had returned from the river to claim her only child, I left the city of Riga behind me, and set off for England.

It was a long, cold journey home, my friends. Without Ilze, I could not afford a carriage or an inn; I dragged myself along the continent's highways, snatching fitful bouts of sleep under trees, in bushes—anywhere I might lie unseen until morning. At first I attempted to beg for alms, but it was as though none could see me. My lack of any language save English, I thought, or the misery writ in my eyes.

I do not remember what I ate, nor where or how I drank, but I crossed that whole lonely land, and the choppy seas which make England an isle. I did these things for you, my dearest friends, for I could not rest easy until I had told you of what happened.

But now I can delude myself no longer—Smilšu māte is calling me, and I must go. For I can admit at last, to myself as well as you, that I did not in fact survive the steamer's wreck, but drowned in the cold, stately waters of the Dagauva along with the Countess of —, all those many miles from home.

But do not despair. Though I am leaving you, whom I have just rejoined, we shall surely meet again. All those who live must cross that river's waters, to die and live again on its most distant shore. And if you ever should see sand in your chambers, or the face of a woman whose eyes are shadow-shrouded, know that I shall see you soon.

*What historical period did you choose and what attracted
you to it?*

The Mother of Sands is set in the 19th century Governate of
Livonia (what is now Latvia). Specifically, significant events
take place in Riga, the capital. I was doing some testing of
my library's new check-out system and looking for a suitably
obscure book that people wouldn't need if I had it checked out
to myself. I picked up a handful of older, more obscure books,
among them one called *The Balts* by Marija Gimbutas. I took
to reading it, of course, and found the section on religion
especially fascinating, with its discussion of sacred groves and
goddess-worship. The name of the Mother of Sands, Smilšu
Māte, really spoke to me, and I set myself to tell a Gothic
ghost story with just a touch of steam, in the tradition of Mary
Shelley's *Frankenstein*.

*What did you change and what do you see the fallout from
it to be?*

Not much is changed in my story, per se. One of the biggest
changes is the mixing of bronze age Baltic goddess-worship
with contemporary Riga, by which time the city was in the
throes of a nationalist revival which included an attempt to
recreate these ancient pagan religious practices. Although
there might not be any direct fallout from the change—at least
until you die—I like how this veers away from the (usually
only implied) Christian cosmology of most Steampunk. As
someone who is not a Christian, I always find myself taken
aback by assumptions authors make about the afterlife, and
the shorthand used to describe it in SFF stories set in our own
world.

What texts were crucial to your research?

The bulk of my research ended up being spent on trying to find more information about The Mother of Sands. In addition to *The Balts,* I hunted down information on short lyrical poems called dainas, and any references I could find which referred to the various mate or "mother" spirits. English-language information about ancient Baltic rites and rituals are thin on the ground, so I also ended up e-mailing several people in Latvia through a mutual acquaintance who gave me what little information they could find, as well.

What is a good introduction to this period?

The Balts is an intriguing (if somewhat dated) introduction to Bronze Age Baltic culture. A more modern text is *Indo-European Poetry and Myth,* by M.L. West, which covers this time period more broadly. For information on the First Latvian Awakening, check out Kristina Jaremko-Porter's chapter in *The Voice of the People,* edited by Matthew Campbell and Michael Perraudin.

1860

NO ONE'S LAND
Anne E. Johnson

Chefchaouen, Morocco

Her father had no idea that Rajae knew how to use his telescope. She'd secretly figured it out six years before, when she was only ten. Whenever she could, Rajae sneaked into her father's office to gaze at the wide triangle of sky between two peaks of the Rif Mountains. The sight of Venus shimmering into view and the red aureole of Mars comforted her and gave her hope.

Lately, though, she angled the telescope lower, training its lens on the edges of the war that closed in on her beloved town of Chefchaouen. Some residents had grown used to the Europeans, even welcoming their "civilizing influences" on society. Some, like her father and his friends, wanted the Europeans out. A group of resistance soldiers met in their cellar, and had started to stockpile guns and explosives. Her father tried to hide this from Rajae and her mother and sisters. But Rajae, always listening, heard everything. The situation, she knew, would soon get worse.

Early one morning she witnessed a horrid fight in the mountains through her telescope. First there were plumes of smoke. The gun blasts reached her ears more slowly, ringing against the mountainside long after the battle had stilled.

That day, as she and Mama cooked, she asked, "Why do the French and Spanish armies fight? Why don't they go home?"

"They want our land," said Mama. She scraped a ball of dough over a flat sieve to make the evening's couscous. "Men need to own things."

"European men?"

Mama's smile hid ten thousand secrets. "No, hayati. All men."

As she walked to market with her sisters that afternoon, Rajae gazed at the green majesty of the surrounding mountains.

"Watch where you're going," her youngest sister, Lati, shouted when Rajae careened into a display of copper plates.

"I'm so sorry," Rajae told the fuming plate vendor.

Lati dragged her away. "What is wrong with you? Did you meet a boy?" Lati's eyes grew wide. "Are you in love? Is he dreamy?"

"What? No." Rajae shook her head at her silly sister. Lati was a bright girl, but not as thoughtful, not as much of a listener as Rajae. "Lati, do you think this is our land?" Rajae waved her arms to indicate the town, the townspeople, the mountains. "Does all this belong to us?"

"Well, yes," Lati replied without hesitating. "Papa says we own this land and the Europeans should leave now. Papa says it's worth everything to fight for our land."

Rajae revised her assessment of Lati: she did listen, but she didn't always think. "I'm just not sure you're right, Lati. Allah made this land. Why should it belong to any of us?"

Lati's eyes grew wide again, this time with fear. "Don't ever let Papa hear you say that."

"I'm not afraid of Papa," Rajae half lied, knowing she'd never tell him she used his telescope. "I think I'll talk to him about this. I don't think he should be fight…"

For an instant, something blocked the sun and turned the market street gray. Scanning the skies, Rajae saw a black object like a giant horse shoe. It seemed much too large to be a bird and much too heavy to fly. Then it zoomed away.

"I have to see this," she said, dropping her basket of oranges.

Lati called after her, "It's gone. There's nothing to see!"

"There is with a telescope," Rajae said. Hitching up the hem of her dress to just above common decency, she ran up the steep incline to the family home.

A recessed back entrance led right to the stairs next to her father's office. Rajae was in such a hurry, she burst open his office door without knocking. It wasn't until her face was pressed to the telescope's eyepiece, that the four men she'd just run past registered in her mind.

They would throw her out the moment she acknowledged them. She knew that. So she kept right on searching the sky for the huge flying horse shoe. What she saw instead was a wisp of purple and green smoke twirling up from the trees on the side of the northern mountain. No cannon or campfire had ever released smoke like that.

Taking a big breath, Rajae pulled her head back from the telescope and turned. As expected, her father and three other businessmen stood around her, gawping. "You can punish me later, Papa," she said before he could get a word out. "Right now, I must go. A huge object fell out of the sky. We should go see whether anyone below it got hurt."

"Rajae?" was all he managed to say by the time she was out the door and clattering down the back steps.

The question was, how to get to the mountainside.

By good fortune, a youth named Mahi was just down the road, driving his family's milk delivery cart. Normally his flirting made Rajae wince, but today she took advantage of his affection.

"Mahi, wait," she called, running toward him. The glint in his eye told her she could get anything she needed. "Let me ride with you."

"Of course, Miss Rajae." He helped her up, but as she climbed the wooden runner board, she made a big show of dropping a bracelet.

"Oh, my gold bangle," she exclaimed, overacting the part. "It fell in the dirt."

"Never fear, habibti."

The moment Mahi set his foot onto the road to retrieve the bracelet, Rajae snatched up the reins and slapped the horses into action. "I'll bring this back," she called over her shoulder to the love-struck milkman. "Keep that bauble as collateral. It's worth more than your cart."

Swallowing down a pang of guilt she led the two horses toward the smoke column at a powerful clip. The road, she was amazed to find, had been widened and improved. Having all those soldiers around at least has one advantage, she thought, ducking under a low-hanging branch as she sped past.

She and the horses were all gasping for breath by the time she reached the source of the brightly colored smoke. The big horseshoe had indeed fallen from the sky. However, nothing seemed to be crushed beneath it. Instead, the huge black structure was itself pouring smoke from one end. Rajae could find no fire, or even damage.

She quickly lost interest in the smoke when a square door at the other end slid open and someone emerged. Or rather something. Rajae had never seen any living creature like this one.

It walked on four legs like a deer, yet its body curved upward beyond those legs, supporting two shorter limbs and a head. It reminded Rajae of a huge scorpion, except that its smooth skin was burgundy lined with black veins. Its wide head was encased in a hinged, lidded bowl of silver and glass.

"Hello," said Rajae. She was mesmerized by the constant, graceful of motion of torso and limb, as if the creature stood on a ship's deck while crossing the choppy sea. "How do you make your building fly?" she asked. "Can you understand me?" Deciding the visitor couldn't speak Arabic, she repeated her question in French and then Spanish.

The strange being touched the casing around its head. The words resonating from the head casing were perfect Darija Arabic. "We need to return home."

Rajae, seeing no mouth, had the sense that it was turning its thoughts directly into sound. "Where is your home?" she asked, trying to pronounce each word clearly.

This time, the visitor didn't wait to answer. "Beyond your view." It pointed straight up through the trees.

"Among the stars?" Rajae's voice caught. "You flew here from out there?"

"Yes. However, we require fuel for our return flight." The creature let its upper limbs ripple like water snakes. "This land contains a mineral similar to the one we use at home for fuel. You call it iron. If you will allow us to remove iron from the stones here, we will repay you with knowledge of worlds beyond this one and also means of traveling to those worlds."

Rajae held her hand to her pounding heart. "That sounds wonderful."

"The Chisars, my people, will also offer much gratitude."

Rajae dipped at the knees, lowering her eyes respectfully. "We humans will be honored to aid the Chisars."

"Perhaps," said the Chisar, "some humans might fly with us to see our world for yourselves."

"Oh!" The thought of getting a chance to fly through space took Rajae's legs out from under her. She grabbed for an oak branch, but missed. Before she sank to the rough ground, the Chisar rushed toward her with steps so smooth it seemed to float.

A single muskets blast came from the road. With its limbs rigid, the Chisar staggered back.

"Stay away from her, Spawn of Satan!" a man shouted in French. A dozen or so French soldiers pushed through the overgrown curtain of leaves, the barrels of their muskets trained on the alien. "Do not move, devil," growled the one with gold brocade on his shoulder.

A lifetime of experience and instinct told Rajae to fear for her virginity. But not one of the soldiers, normally randy and rancid around Moroccan girls, paid Rajae any mind. Even more surprising was the next voice she heard from another direction.

"It's over here, commander," a soldier called out in Spanish. Between the trunks of the cedar trees, Rajae saw flashes of blue and red uniforms. And instead of firing on their rivals, the French commander sent two of his troops to approach, guns down at their sides. They spoke fervently in an awkward hybrid of French and Spanish, glancing and pointing at the Chisar.

Unwilling to trust the fates to make all those men ignore their base natures, Rajae decided it was wise to slink away. After a long glance at the alien to be certain it was unharmed, she slipped between the parting double trunks of an oak tree. But before she could run away, an astonishing sound froze her to her place.

"Over here! Quick, man." It wasn't just Arabic: it was her own father's voice.

Sure enough, he emerged into the clearing, followed by five other men Rajae recognized as occasional guests in their home. Too intrigued to leave the scene, Rajae crouched behind the base of the double tree trunk to watch and listen. That very morning those three groups of men would have blown each other's heads off because of their differences. Now they united against the one who was not like them.

"Where do you come from?" demanded the French commander.

After touching its head casing, the Chisar began to respond in French. "I come from a world far beyond your—"

"What do you want here?" the Spanish commander interrupted, thrusting the bayonet on his rifle to within inches of the alien's chest.

Another touch of its helmet, and the Chisar was able to speak Spanish. "We need minerals from this mountain for fuel. In exchange we can—"

"Never!" shouted the Spaniard. "This land is ours."

The old wounds raged again. Rajae's father cried, "No! It is ours."

Rather than challenging him, the Spanish commander bowed to Rajae's father. A European, bowing to a Moroccan! Rajae had to stop her mouth so they wouldn't hear her gasp.

"I only meant," the Spaniard said in florid, arcane Arabic, "that this land belongs to our species." He indicated the Chisar with a rude toss of his head. "That monster has no right to be here, let alone take our priceless minerals."

Not priceless, thought Rajae. You sell minerals all the time.

The surprises hadn't ended. Rajae's father, the proudest anti-colonialist in the region, shook hands with both the Spanish and the French commanders. "Seize that creature!" her father ordered.

Soldiers from all three groups closed around the Chisar, binding its upper limbs and tying two ropes around its waist as leashes. They led the bewildered alien away, looking like a disfigured red cow. With rude, frantic voices they asked it questions as they tramped up to the road, but it didn't answer.

"You tied its arms, so it can't touch its helmet to speak, you idiots," Rajae growled under her breath. "Not that speaking to you would do it any good."

The thud of boots and the scraping footfalls of the prisoner soon faded. Rajae was left alone in the lively forest silence. Curiosity pulled her out of her hiding place. She wanted to explore the huge ship that could fly. Slowly she climbed around the tree trunk and examined the wall nearest her. It was black metal and of a matte texture, like unglazed ceramic. Rajae ran her fingers along it. Silver or steel would have felt cold. This had no discernible temperature.

Another Chisar appeared on the other side of the airship. Rajae let out a startled cry, but instantly prayed that the soldiers hadn't heard. When no one returned to the clearing, she walked around the aircraft to greet the alien. "I am Rajae."

The Chisar touched its helmet. "I am Neb. My co-familiar, Bebben, was taken against its will."

Ashamed, Rajae bowed her head and clasped her fingers together in supplication. "I am sorry, Ned. Human beings can sometimes be...unreasonable."

Neb bent its four supporting legs, lowering its curved body to the ground. "We need iron."

Looking around to be sure they were alone, Rajae asked, "Why don't you just take the iron? Maybe at night, when no one will see you."

"We cannot. We must have permission from the commanders of this planet."

Rajae grimaced. "You won't like them, and they won't like you."

"I am alone without Bebben. We are trapped here without iron."

Rajae's heart ached. "One of the men who took your friend is my father. I'll try to convince him to release Bebben." She started toward the road. "Stay with your flying ship. You'll be safe in there."

"Thank you, Rajae." Nab crossed its upper limbs in front of its torso, which Rajae read as gratitude and respect.

"It's the least I can do. We humans aren't all bad." Pausing just long enough to be sure Neb had closed itself into its ship, Rajae ran to the milkman's cart and roused the horses into a trot.

She found Mahi and his family outside her house, arguing with her mother.

"Here's your cart!" Rajae called as she leaped out. They rushed toward her, shouting and flailing their arms, but she was too quick. In seconds she was around the house, in the back door, and up the stairs to her father's office.

But her father wasn't there. She wracked her brain, wondering where the newly united forces of Morocco,

France, and Spain would take a prisoner from another world. Scanning the room for clues, her eye fell on the telescope at the window.

I'm turning into quite a spy, she thought, not sure whether to be proud or appalled. Aiming the telescope low, she examined the windows and streets of her own town. It didn't take long to spot the crowd of gesticulating people swarming around the Magistrate's Hall.

Rajae glimpsed a flash of silver and a streak of Burgundy entering the white adobe building. "Bebben!" she gasped. "What will they do to you?"

She paced around the office, clenching her fists, trying to figure out how to help the prisoner. Run to the magistrate and demand to see her father? They would never let her in, and if they did, he'd never listen to her. Sound the klaxon bell and entreat the townspeople for patience and leniency? She wasn't enough of a fool to believe that would work.

Still without a viable plan, Rajae hurried down the back stairs and out to the street.

"Miss Rajae, I really must have an apology for—"

Rajae brushed the milkman's words away "Is this land ours?" she asked him.

"I beg your pardon?"

"Do human beings have the right to say the earth is ours?"

Mahi shrank under her fiery gaze. "Who else would it belong to, miss?" he asked timidly.

Shaking her head, Rajae stepped closer to him. "That's your answer? Why can't people really think about things?"

"But I don't—"

"Who else would to the world belong to, you're wondering? Well, how about to everyone? Or better yet, to no one?"

A man hurried toward them, up the steep main street. It was the butcher, Ahmad Berdugo. He huffed from exertion. "Did you hear the news? They've captured a monster from beyond the stars that wanted to steal our land. We made a truce with the Europeans so we can execute the beast and blow up its magic flying house."

"You're going to execute it?" Rajae's pulse raced.

"Oh, we'll give it a trial," said the butcher with a butcher's bloody grin. "No matter what the French may say, we are not barbarians."

Mahi's family, Rajae's family, and all their neighbors laughed and cheered. They were the ones who seemed like aliens.

Ignoring her mother and Lati calling to her, Rajae tore back to the street near her house. Mahi had abandoned his milk cart to follow the excitement. This time, Rajae didn't feel the slightest guilt about taking his transportation.

She rushed toward the Chisar crash site, her jaw clenched and tears blurring her vision. Maybe I can at least save one of them, she thought over and over. The dirt from the horses' hard-striking hooves stung her cheeks, but she didn't bother pulling her scarf over her face. I deserve this pain, just for being human on this shameful, dreadful day.

The moment she ran down to the clearing from the road, Neb stepped out of the flying ship. "Where is my co-familiar?"

"I could not save Bebben. I am sorry. They are going to kill your friend and then blow up your ship." Frowning at Ned, her fellow oddity, Rajae asked, "How can we get you iron?"

"I cannot take anything from a planet without permission."

Rajae slapped both hands against her breastbone. "I am giving you permission. I've lived on Earth my whole life, so I have as much right as anyone to grant you whatever you need."

After pausing a moment as if it was considering her statement, Neb touched its helmet. "Wait, please." It disappeared into the ship.

Rajae started to pace, but only made a few passes in front of the door before Neb returned. The contraption it held looked similar to a hat rack. "Don't we need something to carry the stones in?" Rajae asked.

"No. This machine will extract the iron."

Rajae cocked her head doubtfully. "If you say so. In any case, we should hurry." Already the voices of townspeople and the clacking of horses grew closer. "Where should we go to gather—?"

"Here." Neb raised the coat rack and then plunged the pointed feet into the ground. Like a thousand mites marching, a rusty red color swarmed up the legs and the central pole. Neb wrapped both its upper limbs around the pole and then, to Rajae's alarm, pressed its torso flat against the red-pulsing metal.

"Don't!" she cried, watching Neb's burgundy skin brighten to a pulsing, glowing cherry hue.

Neb let go of the device and arched its back, absorbing the color and light that sprayed from the machine's surface. Neb's silver helmet reflected the red glow. Its whole body shook.

Rajae believed she was witnessing the alien's death. "What's happening? Is the machine broken? Do you need help?"

Finally, when Neb's seizure reached a violence that would have killed a human, another great change overcame it. Its body grew still and swollen. Neb bent its back so acutely that its head nearly reached its hind quarters.

"Down there!" cried an unwelcome human voice from the upper road.

"Neb, hurry!" Rajae whispered. "Can you hear me? We should go inside your ship." When she tried to approach Neb, the heat radiating from it forced her back. "Neb, please."

But it was too late. A mob of townspeople carrying sticks, swords, and rifles descended into the crash site from all sides. Her father was among them. "Rajae!" he shouted. "Come away from there. Stand behind me."

"No. You'll kill my friend. Swear you won't hurt our guest."

Her father said something, but his words were washed away in the flood of sound Neb emitted. A million trumpets playing at once could not have filled the atmosphere so densely with wailing. And then a path of light grew from Neb's chest. The beam shot out and up; twisting as it rose, it reached over the treetops and around the mountain side.

The wailing stopped short. And as quickly as it had appeared, the light bridge disappeared, a lizard's tongue retracting into its mouth. But the light had brought something with it.

"Bebben!" Rajae hurried toward the other Chisar, who had suddenly appeared and now struggled to find its footing. "How did you get here?" Knowing the answer would take too much time, she turned to more urgent matters. "How do we get the iron into the ship?"

Touching its helmet, Bebben said, "The ship does not require iron. We, the Chisar, require it." Bebben put one upper limb against its co-familiar's chest. "Neb has extracted the iron. Now we have power. We are no longer bound by the physics of this world."

As it pulled the conduit from the ground, Bebben spoke to Neb with incomprehensible syllables. It led the other alien toward the ship.

"Not bound by the physics of this world." Rajae echoed Bebben's words. The glorious concept infused her imagination: An existence without boundaries! Freedom for her mind and body!

The spell broke when her father grasped her waist and pulled her away from the airship. As she came back to herself, Rajae saw the ship's door close. Its black walls turned the color of ripe dates. The air around the ship smelled of burning metal.

Silently, the great horseshoe rose toward the treetops. Struggling in her father's arms, Rajae looked around at the humans she was trapped among. Men, women. Moroccan, French, Spanish. The moment this alien diversion faded from memory, they would all be at each other throats again. All the old wars would continue.

"No, no, no." Rajae turned her head to meet her father's gaze. The rising ship cast a deep shadow over his face, making him look tired and defeated. "I refuse to be bound by the physics of this world," she told him earnestly.

"What? What did you say?"

Once she'd squirmed free, Rajae scrambled to the top of a boulder. She put her head back and roared toward the ship with every fiber of her strength. "Take me with you!"

She saw the beam of light for an instant before it engulfed her. Her arms prickled with warmth as it lifted her, breaking the chains of life as she knew it.

What historical period did you choose and what attracted you to it?
I chose 1860 Morocco, at the time when France, England, and Germany were all fighting to colonize North Africa, without regard to the needs or rights of the Moroccans themselves. I visited Morocco many years ago and found it to be a fascinating and colorful country. The influences from the various European cultures are sometimes blended and sometimes at odds with traditional Moroccan culture.

What did you change and what do you see the fallout from it to be?
I had a spaceship crash in the Rif mountains, causing the various colonial powers to join forces against what they perceive as an alien invasion. I also empowered a young Moroccan woman (something that would not have happened at the time) to stand up against the colonists. The fallout of such an event would (hopefully) be an awareness among European powers that the land was not theirs to take.

What texts were crucial to your research?
Douglas Porch. *The Conquest of Morocco.* New York: Farrar, Straus & Giroux, 2005.

Susan Gilson Miller. *A History of Modern Morocco.* London: Cambridge Univ. Press, 2013.

What is a good introduction to this period?
The Kingdom of Morocco, a BBC documentary.

early 1920s

STEEL SAMURAI
Patrick S. Baker

Three men, killed by simple sword thrusts to the chest, lay in the White Lotus Joy House's waiting room. The bouncer's headless body lay next to the sliding door, half drawn sword at his side, his head a yard away. Blood was splashed everywhere.

Honda Tejo bowed to his senpai, Yanai Kanko, and ushered the investigating yoriki in. Like most brothels in Edo's Floating World, the place had a simple waiting area with a few mats on the floor, some erotic prints on the walls and a visual menu of the pleasures offered for the illiterate and gaijin. Behind a sliding paper-screen door were the pillowing rooms; four on either side of a short corridor.

Kanko and Tejo, both veterans of the Siberian campaign against the Bolsheviks, and hardened policemen, very familiar with gore and death, looked wide-eyed at the sheer level of violence. The two detectives, careful to avoid the blood, tiptoed deeper into the brothel. Each of the private rooms held the same scene, a dead man and women in various stages of undress, all killed with single sword strokes. Only the last room on the right was different; the dead man was a Western foreign barbarian, a gaijin of some kind; the body was large and hairy. The killer or killers had decapitated this victim, and taken his head and also all his clothes. The killer had also murdered the joy girl in this room, too. The two detectives went back to the entrance and Tejo waved in the burakumin clean-up crew.

"What do we know, Tejo?" Kanko asked his kohai as the untouchables went by.

The doshin detective pulled a note book from his short-waisted, Western-styled suit jacket and read: "At about 11:00 tonight, a Hokama Tessai entered the White Lotus and found the four bodies here in the waiting room. He ran to the Omon Gate station and reported this. Komomo Arata Kanjiro and I were dispatched at 11:32 to investigate. We found the place just like you see it. I sent Komomo Arata back to the station to report what we found and to get a patrol here to secure the scene. You arrived at 12:05."

Kanko and Tejo walked along the short path through the front garden and stepped on to the dirt street.

"I will question this Hokama Tessai, fetch him for me," Kanko ordered.

"Yes," Tejo bowed.

Kanko told Senior Patrolman Kugimiya Ryu to start his men questioning any likely witnesses and to let the detective know if they found anything interesting.

Tejo arrived with Hokama Tessai in tow.

Hokama bowed to Kanko.

Kanko politely returned the bow and ordered the man to tell him what had happened.

"Yoriki-Sama, I'm a printer," Hokama started, as he twisted his ink stained hands which testified to the truth of that statement.

"My shop is just outside the Omon Gate. I just finished a big job for some gaijin today and got paid a big bonus. So I thought I'd visit a joy house to celebrate with some pillowing. I have been to the White Lotus before. I looked in and saw the bodies. I ran back to the police station and told the police what I saw."

Kanko merely nodded while Tejo made notes.

"Anything else?"

"Like what, Yoriki-Sama?"

"Did you see anything strange, or out the ordinary?"

"No, nothing like that, Yoriki-Sama."

"Did you do anything else before you came here?"

Hokama pointed to a legless beggar across the road. "Yoriki-Sama, I gave that beggar a mon for luck. He is here every time I visit."

"Thank you," Kanko said to the printer with a curt nod. "Doshin Honda will see you out of the district."

Hokama bowed deeply, feeling lucky he had avoided getting murdered and left quickly with the junior detective.

Kanko strode through the crowd gathering in the dirt street and stood over the legless man. The beggar sat with a sign that read: "Help a veteran. Lost legs at Tsingtao, fighting for the Emperor. May the seven gods of good fortune smile on you!"

"So beteran, you were at Tsingtao?" Kanko asked without preamble.

"Yes, Yoriki-Sama," the man replied and bowed as best he could. "I am No Kinji."

"What regiment?"

"The Forty-Eighth under Colonel Yamashita. I was a lance corporal. A German 150mm shell killed most of my squad, but just took my legs, so I guess Bishamonten smiled on me that day."

"I am Yanai Kanko and I was with the Forty-Eighth in Siberia, as a second lieutenant, until a Borushebiki shot me in the ass," Kanko smiled.

"A sadly too common wound for young officers, of which few people speak," Kinji laughed and Kanko joined in.

"Has any other police spoken to you?"

"No, Yanai-Sama."

Kanko made a mental note to speak to the patrol men about ignoring the obvious witnesses just because they did not want to talk to a possible untouchable.

"You know about the trouble at the White Lotus?"

"Yes, Yanai-Sama," Kinji nodded. "It is a terrible thing that a man cannot do some pillowing without getting murdered."

"Indeed," Kanko nodded. "Did you see anything?"

"Yes, Yanai-Sama, I see many things."

"Anything that might have to do with the murders?"

"Yes, Yanai-Sama," Kinji said suddenly very serious. "I saw a big gaijin go in. That was odd because gaijin usually go to the bigger and better joy houses along Nakanocho Street. Then while I was in the alley relieving myself, a horseless carriage came up to the gate of the White Lotus. That is unusual too because they're hardly any autos in the Floating World. Three samurai got out of the auto and went into the house. Another barbarian stayed in the horseless carriage. A short time later the three samurais came out, one was carrying two cloth sacks, then the carriage took them away."

"You pay close attention to things, No Kinji."

"A crippled man does not live long in the Floating World without keeping his eyes open."

"How'd you know the three men were samurai?"

"They dressed like you, like a gaijin, with a short jacket, and had swords in their obi sashes, like you. Plus they moved like samurai; quick, quiet and watchful."

"If you saw them again could you identify them?"

"No, Yanai-Sama, they wore hats which shaded their faces."

"Tell me about the horseless carriage."

"It carried the four men and was mainly black, but with red doors and it smoked and stank."

"How about the foreigner driving the auto?" Kanko asked. "Could you recognized him, No Kinji?"

"No, Yanai-Sama," the old veteran shook his head. "All gaijin look alike to me."

"Indeed and thanks, No Kinji," Kanko dropped a silver isshuban coin into the beggar's bowl and left.

Kanko walked back to the White Lotus, through the much thinner crowd, most people moving off seeking other amusements. Tejo returned and Kanko told his kohai about the interview with No Kinji and then told the younger man to put out a message to the patrols to look for the auto. Tejo rushed off to carry out his orders.

A large automobile painted black and white pulled up just as Tejo returned to the area. Kanko approached the auto, Tejo also approached but stayed behind his senpai. Inside the horseless carriage were Imamura Izo, Chief of the Omon Gate Station and Kanko's direct superior, with Imamura were Machi-Bugyo Sakai Torio, Edo's police commissioner, directly appointed by the Shogun, and an unknown man. Kanko bowed deeply to his superiors. Imamura waved Kanko closer through the open window. As he stepped up, Kanko quickly studied the stranger. He was an average looking man of indeterminate age, dressed like Kanko, but instead of a katana and revolver, he had a katana and a traditional wakizashi short sword. Pinned to the stranger's lapel was a small, white chrysanthemum emblem, the symbol of the Emperor's direct service.

"How goes the investigation of the murders at the White Lotus?" Imamura asked without preamble.

"We are just starting, Imamura-Sama," Tejo said, carefully not looking at the stranger. "I was about to go to the station to write my first report."

"Yes," Imamura said. "Don't worry about the report right now. But once you finish it bring it directly to me. The investigation into the gaijin's death is over. Is that clear, Kanko?"

"Yes, Imamura-Sama," Kanko and Tejo both bowed deeply as the auto drove away.

"Imperial Shinobi Oniwaban?" Kanko asked.

"Yes," Tejo responded. "I think so, too. The gaijin's murder?"

"Indeed," Kanko said. "How did the honorable Imamura even know a barbarian was murdered and why was an imperial secret service man with him?"

"That is politics and as police we don't worry about politics," Tejo said. "We are obedient to the will of the Emperor expressed through the Shogun."

"Of course," Kanko agreed. "We will not investigate the foreigner's death. But the other murders, the customers, the joy girls, we will continue to investigate."

"Yes," Tejo said and bowed.

Senior Patrolman Kugimiya Ryu came up to the detectives with a junior patrolman.

"Sirs," Kugimiya bowed. "Patrolman Maeno Jo has found the horseless carriage."

"Show us!" Kanko ordered.

The junior patrolman led his seniors, walking at a brisk pace through the crush of street performers, joy girls, kabuki dancers and artists that inhabited the twisted alleys and mud streets of Edo's Floating World. The auto was parked in a trash-filled alley between a saki bar, called the Blue Devil, and an even cheaper joy house than the White Lotus, called the Green Koi Pond.

"Stay here," Kanko ordered the others as he handed his katana and pistol to Tejo. The senior detective loosened his cravat and pulled his shirttail out to cover his obi. While the rest of the group slid back into the shadows, Kanko walked like a drunk man passed the red and black horseless carriage. As he went by the automobile, Kanko looked carefully through the windows. A still liquid dark spot, which Kanko recognized as drying blood, stained the backseat. In the front passenger seat sat a leather bag of tools with some Western writing on it and a white chrysanthemum emblem stamped on it. Kanko quickly circled back to his fellow police.

"That is the automobile," Kanko said as he re-tied his cravat, straightened his clothing and took back his weapons. "Tejo, go to the Green Koi Pond and see if anyone there knows anything about the auto. I'll go into the Blue Devil and check there. Kugimiya and Maeno stay here. If either Tejo or I shout, come in hard and fast."

Kanko watched Tejo enter the Green Kio Pond and then he entered the Blue Devil. The saki bar was a tawdry place even for the Floating World. No decorations hung on its plain wooden walls, not even tasteless erotic prints. The bar had just a few cheap bamboo tables, mismatched wicker and wooden chairs, all set well away from each other. There was no sense of conviviality, or friendship, in the place. At the Blue Devil, all the customers wanted to do was get drunk and do it alone. The bartender was a small, rat-faced man, missing the little finger on his left hand, from that Kanko knew he was yakuza. The gangster-barman eyed the detective and then shot a look to the only gaijin in the place. Kanko gave him the tiniest of nods.

Kanko went up to the barbarian. If the number of empty and overturned saki bottles on the table was any sign, the foreigner was very drunk. The gaijin was a large man with a shaved head. As Kanko approached the foreigner looked his way. Kanko saw the gaijin had a huge yellow mustache which drooped over his mouth. The policeman stopped and gave the foreigner a polite, medium-deep bow.

"Zur," Kanko said in English. "I am Senior Detective Yanai Kanko. I would…"

The barbarian leapt from his seat and punched Kanko in the jaw. The detective staggered back, ears ringing and spots before his eyes. The gaijin raised his fist again. The yakuza barman jumped over the bar, wooden club in hand. The gangster covered the distance to the gaijin in two hops and struck the barbarian at the seam of his neck and shoulder. The huge man fell to his knees with a grunt and then toppled over. The barbarian started to retch as his head hit the floor.

The barman ordered two of the patrons to sit the gaijin up in a chair so he wouldn't drown in his own vomit, then he helped Kanko to a seat.

Tejo entered the bar. He saw what was happening, shouted out the door for help as he drew his revolver and ordered everyone to stand still. Kugimiya and Maeno burst in the door also with pistols drawn.

Kanko shook his head to clear the buzzing and quickly explained the situation. Tejo let all the customers leave without taking their names. The barman said his name was Ohishi Rei while he locked the doors, gave the police a bucket of water. The yakuza then leaned against the bar, arms crossed and watched the proceedings with cold, dead eyes.

The patrolmen handcuffed the gaijin to the only sturdy chair in the place and dumped the bucket of water over his head. He came to sputtering and cursing in a language that sounded something like English but was not.

"Does anyone know what he is going on about?" Kanko asked.

"It is German," Tejo said. "I studied it in school, but he is going very fast and some of what he is saying makes no sense. He is saying something about us, 'flat-faced monkeys', killing his 'korpsbruder', that mean 'corps brother', or close comrade. How could we, 'yellow bastards', kill his friend, after the Emperor send them here to help the Emperor? See, I said it made no sense."

"Ask him his name, and tell him we are the police and we are trying to find the men who killed his friend," Kanko ordered Tejo.

Tejo stepped up, slapped the babbling gaijin hard on the top of his head to get him to shut up. Then, speaking slowly and clearly, the junior detective addressed the now quiet foreigner.

The gaijin said nothing, but his eyes darted around the room. Kanko told Maeno Jo to fetch the bag of tools from the horseless carriage. Kanko poured the implements out of the bag onto a table and quickly sorted them by size. The detective was no mechanic, but he recognized the tools were well-made and carefully maintained. Among all the instruments stamped with outlandish writing, Kanko found one stamped 'Daido' in kanji script with a stylized chrysanthemum.

Kanko smiled thinly as he suddenly realized at least part of what was going on.

"Tejo," Kanko said. "Ask the German his name again and then him we know he is using his mechanical and engineering skills to help our Emperor and that his dead friend was doing the same thing. Then tell him we know he drove the automobile when the Imperials killed his friend and all those people at the White Lotus."

Again, speaking slowly and choosing his words carefully, Tejo told the German what his superior said. The German's eyes narrowed and widened as Tejo spoke.

"Ich bin Helmut Weiss," the gaijin said at last and then suddenly started to weep and babble again.

"He says," Tejo translated. "That he did drive the automobile, but he did not know they were going to kill his friend, Hans. They said they were going to pay him off and let him go home."

"Tell Helmut Weiss, that we know he didn't want to help those men kill his friend, but they lied to him," Kanko said. "Then say that if he helps us now by showing us where the killers are, we will see they are punished. Also, I'll personally see he gets back to Germany. My word as a samurai and a man of the Shogun."

As Tejo spoke, Helmut Weiss nodded and said, "Ja, Ja."

The patrolmen released the German and walked him out the door.

"Ohishi Rei," the senior detective said as he moved to leave. "Why did you help with the gaijin?"

"A dead police man would be bad for business," the yakuza man said, raising his left hand and wagging the stump of his little finger. "My oyabun would not like it and I can't afford to apologize many more times."

"Yes," Kanko nodded and tossed the barman a small gold isshuban coin. "For your troubles."

The yakuza bowed as the police detective left.

Outside, Weiss wanted to drive the police in the automobile, but the machine would attract too much unwanted attention. Instead, the detectives walked alongside the gaijin while the two patrolmen walked behind. To anyone in the street, the group looked like three carousers being escorted out of the Floating World by two police.

As they marched along Weiss alternated between babbled on in his barbaric language while Tejo nodded and silently weeping. Kanko preferred the weeping, but quiet, gaijin.

In about ten minutes, Weiss pointed to a whitewashed, windowless warehouse, surrounded by saki and beer bars, joy houses, tattoo parlors, erotic art studios and low-rent kabuki theaters.

As they watched the suspect building, Tejo asked Weiss something.

The German spoke clearly and slowly, now completely sober and in control of himself.

"He says that is the place where he worked and where he dropped off the killers before he drove away to the Blue Devil," Tejo translated and paraphrased Weiss's reply. "He says there are armed guards inside, but he does not know how many, but some. Also there something he calls the 'steel warriors', or maybe the 'war-machines'. Those phrases make no sense to me."

"Well, nothing to be gained by standing here," Kanko declared after a moment.

The senior detective disheveled himself again and gave his sword and revolver to Tejo. He then made a quick circuit of the whitewashed building and returned.

"Tejo, take Weiss to the Omon Gate station and put him in a one-man lockup for safe-keeping. Then tell Imamura-sama what we have found and that we need the Heavy Flying Squad to enter the building. Senior Patrolman Kugimiya, keep your patrolmen away from this area, but collect them out of sight of here in case they are needed for the arrests. I spotted two entrances, a door for people and a loading dock. I will be at the northwest corner, across the street but someplace I can observe both entrances. Tejo, find me there when you get back. Does everyone understand?"

The other men all bowed, including Weiss. Kanko took his weapons back from Tejo, before the junior detective lead the cooperative gaijin away. Kanko tucked the katana down his pants leg to hide it. He then slipped his revolver around to the small of his back so it was hidden by his jacket and half-limped, half staggered to an observation spot. Two other men, dead drunk, lay sprawled in the same area in front of a beer bar. Kanko joined them.

A few people walked over and around the three men slumping men without taking any notice of them. One stepped over Kanko's legs and then with a quick backhand, thumped the policeman on the head with a small jutte club. Kanko flopped forward as his attacker and another man grabbed his arms and dragged him across the street into the whitewashed building.

Kanko came to, tied to a chair, facing a long table with a foreigner's decapitated head at the far end. Next to the head was Kanko's katana and pistol. The Shinobi Oniwaban agent from the police commissioner's auto sitting next to the head, his hand on Kanko's sword.

"Awake, Yanai Kanko?" the Imperial agent asked.

"Yes," Kanko shook his head to clear his vision.

"I am Amaya Ken and I am disappointed in you, Yanai-sama. What kind of samurai are you, to not obey the orders of your superior? I was there when you were ordered to not investigate the gaijin's death."

"That is so," Kanko said. "But, I was investigating the deaths of the girls, the bouncer and the Japanese customers, not the gaijin. So I find it easy to bear up under your displeasure."

"Clever on your part and clever on your bosu's part too, couching the orders that way," Ken stood. "Let me show you some things, clever detective, and see if you can work out what is going on."

A man built like a sumo wrestler sliced the Kanko's bindings, lifted him out of the chair by his jacket collar and then half pushed, half dragged the detective along as they followed Ken.

The Imperial agent led the trio into a cavernous room. Kanko counted at least six guards, armed with German submachine guns, patrolled in pairs.

Standing along the walls were huge, double man-sized and finely made sets of samurai armor, lacquered black and red with a white chrysanthemum symbol on the chests. Along each arm of the suits was a small cannon fed by a belt from a backpacked ammunition hopper. Two men were working inside one of the sets of armor. The ammo storage was removed and the back swung open like a door. Kanko could see the space was just large enough for a man to stand and a there was a set handles and nobs in a metal box to the front of the space. Kanko realized that was what Weiss had been on about. The armor was not armor that a person wore, but was a machine that a man operated like driving an auto.

"So Yanai Kanko," Amaya Ken said after a moment. "Any idea what is happening?"

"It is a coup," Kanko said. "You and your imperial agents are going to use these war-machines to remove the Shogunate and give that infantile Taisho real power."

"Not a coup, but a restoration of rightful power to the Emperor," Amaya Ken roared. "Also, do not insult the Emperor again!"

The sumo wrestler smacked Kanko on the top of the head so hard it drove the detective to his knees.

"It is no insult to tell the truth," Kanko said mildly as he stood. "Even if it is unpleasant."

"How did you know about the plan?"

"You Imperials are arrogant pigs," Kanko went on. "Striding around with your flower badges, like anyone with half a brain wouldn't notice you. That is no way to keep anything secret. You even mark the tools of your mechanics with it."

Kanko nodded at the war-machines.

"Also, these war-machines, again with the flower emblems, why else would they be in Edo, but to seize power from the Shogun. These things are not from Japan, so you have gaijins, the Germans, helping construct them. One of them was about to betray you, or wanted more money, or something like that. So you lured him to the joy house with promises you would let him go home with lots money. But your assassins killed him and the rest of the people at the White Lotus. Then you lost your other gaijin engineer after you killed the first. I found Weiss and spoke to him, he was very willing to talk, knowing what you did to his friend."

"You are indeed astute," the imperial agent said in honest admiration. "The gaijin we executed was a German engineer named Hans Kleinbauer, he worked with the gaijin, Weiss, who ran away like a coward. We had a problem with the power systems of the steel samurais which Hans Kleinbauer solved, but he wanted more money to finish the job. It was easier to execute him and take the plans for the repair than to pay him."

"So you're working with the barbarian emperor?" Kanko asked. "In exchange, Emperor Taisho has promised to give back Tsingtao to the Germans?"

"Of course," Amaya Ken said. "Or at least, that is what the Germans think."

The large dock door exploded inward, showering the room with wood fragments and knocking everyone off their feet.

Kanko came quickly, if unsteadily, to his feet, as a squad of police armed with American Thompson sub-machine guns rushed in, firing from the hip. The Imperial guards, still stunned by the blast, were quickly cut down. Kanko stepped over to the sumo wrestler, laying dazed on the floor and gave him a solid kick to the head and then started looking for Amaya Ken.

The steel samurai that the mechanics had been working on sprang to life and started firing back at the police. The heavily armed police of Flying Squad scattered and ran from the sudden, unexpected assault. Kanko knew at once Ken was driving the war-machine.

The steel samurai turned to aim at Kanko. The detective dove behind a heavy metal workbench and scuttled away like a crab, as heavy bullets started punch holes in his cover. Kanko pulled himself up along the wall between two of the war-machines and drew his legs up.

Four policemen wheeled an Oerlikon 20mm clip-fed cannon through the blasted loading dock doors and started to fire. The shells knocked Ken's armored suit back and down, but couldn't penetrate the metal skin. When the cannon crew paused to reload, Ken counterattacked, killing the gun crew with a spray of fire.

The steel samurai strode by the hiding Kanko, heading toward the Oerlikon gun. The detective peaked out from his hiding place to see the steel samurai pass by and noticed the war-machine's door was slightly ajar. Ken in his haste had not locked it. Kanko stepped gingerly out and then jumped to just behind the armored suit. He reached up and swung the door completely open. Kanko jumped up, braced his feet on the door jam and at the same time wrapped his arms around Ken's head and neck and pulled. He and Ken shot back out of the war-machine and landed on the concrete floor.

Smacking down on the hard surface knocked the breath out of the detective and loosened his grip on the imperial agent. Ken quickly rolled away and stood up. Then he stepped over to Kanko and feebly kick him. He then kicked again, this time stronger. Kanko curled into a ball covering his head with his hands as he tried to protect himself.

A hand grenade aimed at the now unmoving armor exploded, staggering Ken. Kanko came up into a crouch and lashed out with his right foot, connecting with the imperial's shin and dropped him to his knees. Kanko stood to deliver a punch when Honda Tejo appeared behind Ken and with one slash of his katana removed the imperial's head.

"Tejo!" Kanko shouted and gasped. "I wanted to question him."

"Look at his hand," Tejo said breathless.

Kanko looked down. Clutched in Ken's fist was a small German automatic pistol.

"Domo arigato, Tejo-sama," Kanko bowed to his junior. "You have saved my life."

"Indeed," Tejo said and bowed back. "I had to, who else will help me write the report on this mess."

What historical period did you choose and what attracted you to it?
The late Shogunate period of Japan. I selected the time period because I haven't seen any alt-history stories that took place there. It is always fun to walk untrodden ground.

What did you change and what do you see the fallout from it to be?
The shogunate has survived into the 1920s and is involved in a cold war with Imperial Germany, which survived World War One. Now, imperial agents are attempting to overthrow the Shogun and restore the Emperor to power. Shogunate Japan forms a partnership with expansive American against Imperial Germany and Bolshevik Russia.

Which texts were crucial to your research?
A History of Japan, 1582–1941: Internal and External Worlds by L. M. Cullen and *The End of the Shoguns and the Birth of Modern Japan* by Lawrence J. Zwier and Mark E. Cunningham

What is a good introduction to this period?
Voices of Early Modern Japan: Contemporary Accounts of Daily Life During the Shogun, Constantine Nomikos Vaporis

1952

FATHER RUSSIA
Daniel M. Kimmel

Trofim Lysenko had been expecting the call. Sitting in his well-appointed office as the director of the Lenin All-Union Academy of Agricultural Sciences, he put aside the paper he was revising on increasing crop yields. He had had some time to prepare himself and was ready to act. He listened to the caller, took in the information calmly, and gave the necessary orders. Then, without a trace of emotion crossing his gaunt features, and with his slicked down hair remaining plastered to his scalp, he calmly hung up the phone.

Comrade Stalin had suffered a stroke just days before. Though trusted physicians had applied leeches and had given him the very best in Soviet medical care, everyone knew it was only a matter of time. As soon as Lysenko learned that the General Secretary was deemed near death, he issued instructions that the body was to be brought to the special facility he had set up at Stalin's behest on the top floor of the Academy. Lysenko wasn't sure that his agronomic theories of grafting and transplants could be applied to humans, but he refused to even consider questioning his patron who firmly believed otherwise.

While the bourgeois "geneticists" scoffed at Lysenko's papers on how plants could be altered by such procedures, leading to new species inheriting the traits of the grafts, Stalin had offered him his unqualified support. Indeed, Stalin had provided more than mere lip service. Lysenko's critics quickly found themselves imprisoned if they were lucky, and executed if they were not. There was no more room for dissenting "western" views in Soviet science than there had been in economics or agricultural policy. Lysenko had cast his lot first with Lenin, then with Stalin, knowing that the leadership of the state always had the best interests of the Soviet proletariat at heart. Let the West embrace Darwin. He had Stalin. In spite of disastrous crops and the occasional massive purge, the Soviet Union and Stalin had persevered through hard times, including the Great Patriotic War, always with Lysenko's unwavering support. The scientist's loyalty had been amply rewarded with power, prestige, and the disappearance of anyone daring to raise a voice in opposition.

Now with the news that Stalin was dying, Lysenko knew he had to move quickly. He had made it clear that he couldn't perform the procedure himself. He was an agronomist, after all, not a surgeon. Due to the complexity of what was likely to be a several hours long operation, two doctors were already in the operating room when Lysenko arrived, along with nurses and an anesthesiologist. One body was being prepared on the operating table already in the room, while a second table—with Stalin's massive form draped in sheets—was being wheeled in.

"Comrades," said Lysenko, "let us begin."

With great fear and trepidation, the senior surgeon moved forward and after a moment's hesitation began the laborious process of detaching the head of the leader of the Soviet Union.

Although he would never have expressed them aloud, Lysenko had had his doubts. Nonetheless he kept his faith in Stalin and the necessity for party discipline, and accepted the possibility that Stalin's scientific instincts were even greater than his own. One evening he and Comrade Stalin and had shared a vodka or three while listening to recordings of the confessions of the fascist geneticists recanting their beliefs, admitting that plants could inherit and pass on the traits of species which had been grafted to them. As he heard so many of these bourgeois researchers confessing to the error of their ways, Lysenko knew he had stayed on the one true and enlightened path. With Stalin's support he had become the leading pioneer for the glorious future for Soviet science. For a number of years now he had set the standards for biological research, ensuring the country would not be sidetracked by the snares of western pseudoscience. However even he had to admit that the grafting of animal parts was far beyond anything he had ever done in the laboratory.

On that fateful night, Comrade Stalin had listen patiently as Lysenko explained what he felt he could do and what was beyond the limits of current experimentation. Yet Stalin insisted that what worked for grain would work for humans. Lysenko finished his glass of vodka and kept his doubts to himself. He had not survived thus far by taunting the bear to its face. He placed his faith in his leader, and hoped that when the time came, if it should come, things would work out for the best. Thus the arrangements had been made.

As expected, the surgery took several hours. The two surgeons moved with speed and skill as they took Stalin's head and carefully grafted it onto the neck of a much younger and healthier body. The body was, in fact, that of one of Lysenko's many critics, and he had been kept safely in a cell in Lubyanka prison where he may have wondered why he was being treated with such care. Shortly before the arrival of Comrade Stalin, the dissident was brought to the hospital and quickly dispatched. His head was summarily disposed of, as he wouldn't be needing it any longer. While the body was stabilized and secured, Stalin's head was being prepared for the transplant

By mid-evening Stalin—which is to say, Stalin's head and his new body—was taken off to a post-op recovery room. The operation had been deemed a success by the surgeons but now Lysenko had to wait and see if the graft took. Would Comrade Stalin regain consciousness? And if he did so, would he be himself, or would the combined trauma of death and radical surgery be too much? Time would tell.

It was at 2 a.m. the following morning when Lysenko found himself roused from a sound sleep in his private office. He had had the couch installed in his suite claiming he had to be welcoming to Party officials when they came, from time to time, to discuss his work. In fact, few did but the couch had proven useful in other ways, including providing a place for him to sack out.

The blond orderly, who couldn't have been much older than eighteen or nineteen, looked fearful as he approached Lysenko's sleeping form. He felt as if he had been caught between a rock and a hard place. In a way, he had.

"Comrade Lysenko, I apologize for waking you, but Comrade Stalin insists on seeing you at once." He kept his head bowed in the hopes that, if he did not make eye contact, perhaps the scientist wouldn't remember him afterwards

It took a moment for the leading light of modern Soviet science to rouse himself from his slumber and process the message he was being given but then he shook off the drowsiness and rose to his feet. Donning his glasses he turned to the cringing youth and patted him on the shoulder. "You did the right thing, of course. You are to be commended. Take me to Comrade Stalin at once."

The man breathed a sigh of relief and then headed for the exit. "If you will follow me, Comrade?"

Lysenko accompanied the aide down a corridor and up two flights of stairs. Two Red Army soldiers, fully armed, were standing outside the secure room. Lysenko was admitted at once. Already there were several members of his inner circle. He immediately recognized the cherubic face of first deputy Georgy Malenkov, whose beaming smile suggested the news was good, in spite of the beads of sweat on his brow. Next to him was the grandfatherly deputy prime minister Nikolai Bulganin. Lysenko had had less contact with him than with Malenkov, but he knew him to be a highly decorated military man, and part of Stalin's inner circle.

The third person in the room gave Lysenko pause. It was deputy premier Lavrenti Beria. Thin-lipped, balding and wearing his trademark rimless round spectacles, he might have easily been ignored as just another apparatchik doing the bidding of others. In fact, Beria cultivated the image of being a harmless bureaucrat to put people at their ease. Then they might forget he was the second most powerful man in the Soviet Union, the person in charge of the state security services, which he had helped shape to his own liking. Those who had thus misjudged him included Lysenko's late rivals.

While Lysenko was adjusting to be awoken and suddenly thrust into the inner circle of Soviet leadership, Stalin, who was propped up into a sitting position on his hospital bed, was all smiles. Stalin's complexion was still grayish, but was already looking ruddier than when Lysenko had last seen him conscious a few days ago. At the dictator's gesture, the scientist approached the bed.

"Comrade Lysenko, you have truly earned your reputation as the People's Scientist today. I cannot believe how strong I feel." Stalin was all smiles. He seemed more like a man who had just survived an arduous hike rather than one who had come through a revolutionary surgical procedure.

Lysenko beamed at the praise but was not quite ready to pronounce the operation a success. "The Soviet Union has been spared the loss of its great leader, and I am grateful for whatever small part I may have played in that," he said with what he hoped was not too obvious false humility. "To ensure the success of the procedure, I encourage you not to rush back into action, but instead to allow your body to heal and become accustomed to its new role serving the head of state."

The others gasped at Lysenko's phrasing, but Stalin burst out laughing. "Very good, Comrade Lysenko, very good. You have, indeed, literally preserved the head of state. It is this body that needs to make the appropriate adjustments."

"I was wondering about that," said Bulganin. "Where exactly did this body come from?"

"Comrade Beria played the key role in that regard," said Lysenko, knowing that it never hurt to praise the man who ran the NKVD and had a long memory. It was always better to have Beria as an ally.

"It was nothing," replied Beria, echoing Lysenko's protestations of modesty. "We have kept several prisoners well-fed and in good health knowing this situation might arise."

"But whose body was it?" asked Bulganin.

"I'm not sure," interrupted Stalin, making a show of lifting up the bed sheet and examining his new torso, "but I think he was Jewish."

Beria and Bulganin laughed, and after a moment they were joined by Malenkov and Lysenko, as the full implication of Stalin's remark became clear.

"And, I assure you," said Lysenko, "all parts should prove to be in perfect working order."

"That is good," said the smiling leader to Lysenko before turning to the others. "Once I am recovered, I am eager to get on with the rest of Comrade Lysenko's plan."

At this the Politboro members turned on the scientist. It was Beria who put the question to him. "Comrade Lysenko, precisely what other plans do you have for our leader?"

Lysenko was somewhat embarrassed at the attention but since it was an opportunity to expound on the scientific theory that had become renowned as "Lysenkoism" he took the opportunity to lecture his colleagues. "As you know, comrades, my work has been in agriculture and the hybridization of plants. Today, under the inspiration and direction of our leader, we have witnessed the first time my theories have been successfully applied to human beings, making Comrade Stalin, truly, the New Soviet Man."

"Yes, yes," said Beria. "We get that. The operation was a great success. Once Comrade Stalin has fully recovered, what further work needs to be done?"

Lysenko began to warm up to his subject. "Grafting is only the first step of the process, Comrades. The next step is for the hybrid to pass along its dominant traits to the next generation. In the case of Comrade Stalin in his newly invigorated body, it will involve producing a number of children who will have Stalinism in their blood."

"Just think, Comrades," said the dictator, "in just a generation I could be moved to yet another body while the Politboro will be made up entirely of those carrying my thinking in their blood, their brains, and their very bones. We would no longer need to test for Party loyalty. We would know it as a matter of science."

There was a moment of silence as the men contemplated this, and then Beria said, "You know, Comrades, I think we should allow our leader to rest and recuperate. After all," he added with a sly grin, "he will have many fields to plow on behalf of the proletariat."

After a pause Stalin joined in the merriment. "And this time I will select women especially chosen for their task, rather than leave it to chance. At last, I shall have children worthy of the name Stalin."

Three hours later Lysenko was awoken by the aide again, shortly before dawn. It was beginning to become a habit. He was torn between giving him a medal for his diligence to duty and having him taken out and shot. Perhaps there was a way he could do both.

"Yes, what it is?"

"Comrade Lysenko, come quickly. There's been a terrible accident."

Lysenko rushed to Stalin's recovery room. There he saw Comrades Beria, Malenkov and Bulganin standing at an open window. Stalin was nowhere to be seen. "Where is Comrade Stalin?" demanded the chief Soviet scientist.

"Comrade Lysenko, I regret to report a terrible tragedy has befallen us and all the Soviet peoples," replied Beria.

"Terrible," echoed Malenkov.

"Completely unforeseeable," put in Bulganin.

"What is it?"

They stood aside from the window and Lysenko cautiously approached. Several stories below, in the courtyard, there appeared to be a fire. The scientist didn't like the looks of it but he wasn't sure what he was seeing. Stepping back he stared at the three officials with a quizzical look on his face.

"Comrade Stalin wanted a breath of fresh Russian air," explained Malenkov. "He leaned too far out and must have suddenly lost his equilibrium as he toppled over the sill and landed head first on the pavement."

"Of course no one is blaming you," said Beria. "Your operation worked perfectly."

"Flawlessly, one might say," added Bulganin.

"There might still be a way to salvage this," began Lysenko, as the other three exchanged looks that could only be described as fearful. "Even if Comrade Stalin's head was destroyed in the fall, we might still be able to graft all or part of the rest of his body onto another subject."

"Yes, we thought of that," began Beria, removing his spectacles and idly cleaning them with his handkerchief. "Unfortunately it will not be possible."

"Why not?" Lysenko was confused. Something about this scene didn't make any sense.

"By the most unfortunate coincidence, the hearse containing the rest of Comrade Stalin's remains was departing just as he fell from the window."

"I don't understand," said Lysenko although he was beginning to understand all too well.

"At the very moment the body landed on the pavement, the car crashed into it and set off an explosion," said Malenkov.

"Hence the flaming wreckage below," added Bulganin. "It appears we have lost both the head and the body."

"The odds against such a thing happening must have been astronomical," added Beria. "If I believed in the Orthodox Church of my mother I might be tempted to say it was the hand of God."

"Instead," said Malenkov quickly, "it was the hand of Comrade Stalin himself, pushing himself too far out the window, intoxicated by the freedom of our ongoing revolution."

The four men were silent for several moments, and then Beria moved to the window to close it.

"Then Comrade Stalin is dead for good," said Lysenko. "I may be a great scientist but not even I can perform miracles."

Bulganin seemed to heave a sigh of relief but stern looks from the other two cut it short. Instead he shared the look of somber regret with the other men. No one seemed to know what to say. Finally Malenkov broke the silence. "I will be stepping up to succeed Comrade Stalin as chairman of the Council of Ministers. Comrade Beria will be drawing up plans on how to break this sad news to the people and to the world. It goes without saying that we will not be disclosing your operation, Comrade Lysenko. I trust we will have your full cooperation in this matter?"

Lysenko snapped to attention. What he said next could determine his future. "Comrades, my grief knows no bounds, but let me assure you that my loyalty to the Soviet state is firm and should remain unquestioned. As far as I am concerned, the events leading up to today's tragic loss never happened. As to those who performed the actual procedure..."

"Don't worry about them," said Beria, quietly. "It's already been taken care of."

"Comrades, we each have our work to do," said Malenkov. "Comrade Lysenko, if I might have a moment of your time?"

Beria and Bulganin withdrew to attend to whatever assignments they had been given. When the door closed Malenkov turned to Lysenko. "I can't say I have followed your work as closely as Comrade Stalin, but it's clear that your scientific advances have led us in great strides against the decadent West."

Lysenko was not sure where this was going, but he was well aware that Stalin's death meant he needed a new patron. "All my work has been dedicated to the betterment of the Soviet people," he replied, hoping that this was a safe response.

"Yes, of course it has," said Malenkov. "And I was impressed in how far-reaching your work with Comrade Stalin was. Certainly ensuring continuity of leadership is an important goal for the continuing success of our revolutionary policies."

Lysenko may have been a scientist but he hadn't survived as long as he had by having a tin ear for politics. He quickly grasped the direction of the conversation. "Comrade Malenkov pardon, Comrade Chairman Malenkov...please be assured of my loyalty to the Soviet State and to you as its new leader. Whatever my humble scientific research has to offer is completely at your disposal for the good of the people."

Malenkov embraced him in an unexpectedly warm bear hug. "I knew I could count on you, my friend. We shall be seeing a lot of each other in the months and years ahead."

"I shall consider myself fortunate," replied Lysenko as Malenkov showed him to the door.

"I'm just going to tidy up in here. We don't want any state secrets falling into the wrong hands, after all," he said with a conspiratorial chuckle.

Lysenko headed back to his office, mopping his brow with his handkerchief and patting his hair back into place. Stalin's death had put them all in a precarious position and until the dust settled it would be smart to be cooperative and vague with everyone. It probably wouldn't hurt for him to do a similar cleaning of his own, burning whatever notes he had on preparations for the operation. Lack of evidence didn't always prevent a finding of guilt under Soviet justice, but there was no reason to make things easier for any would-be persecutors. When Lysenko entered his office he was surprised to see he was not alone. Comrade Bulganin was waiting for him having already made himself at home on the couch.

"I was hoping to have a word with you," said Bulganin as he rose.

The startled Lysenko quickly recovered. "Of course. How may I be of service to you?"

"As you may know, I am in line to become Secretary of Defense. It is a key position in the government, one that was previously held by Comrade Stalin himself."

"Then even amidst our tears of sorrow for our fallen leader, there is cause for congratulations. I have no doubt you will be a worthy successor to the man who led us through the Great Patriotic War."

"Yes," agreed Bulganin, obviously eager to move beyond the boilerplate that took up so much time in official conversation. "I have to say, I am most intrigued by your experiments, Comrade Lysenko, particularly in how they might be adapted and applied in the defense of our homeland."

"That is always uppermost in my mind, Comrade Bulganin…I mean, Comrade Secretary Bulganin…feeding our people, particularly those who serve in defense of it, can have no higher priority. I hope to increase crop yields in our next five year plan…"

"Yes, I'm sure you do," said Bulganin, whose interests clearly laid somewhere beyond those wheat fields. "However I was thinking more in terms of how to ensure the stability of our leadership, so that we may enjoy continuity in our policies and strategies against our enemies in the West. It does us no good if one person plots and plans the organization of our defenses, and then someone new comes along with no understanding, and who wastes time starting all over again." He paused. "If you get my meaning…"

Lysenko, who had never served in the military, snapped to attention and saluted Bulganin. "Of course you have my complete loyalty and support. Anything to strengthen and preserve our worker's paradise."

Bulganin beamed. "I knew I could count on you, Comrade Lysenko. All I ask for now is that you keep this conversation between just the two of us. We don't want others to leap to false conclusions."

"Those who leap to false conclusions are enemies of the state," responded Lysenko smartly, knowing that that could apply to his own opponents as well as Bulganin's.

"I'm so glad we had this conversation. We must talk again soon. I suspect we have much to share. Perhaps you would enjoy a few days at my dacha as a respite from all your hard work."

"I am entirely at your disposal Comrade Defense Secretary."

A smiling Bulganin departed leaving Lysenko alone in the office. The scientist began to gather the materials that needed to be placed in secured storage or otherwise be destroyed. It took a while as he had taken to scattering the material around his office as a security precaution. The key to locating the documents and fitting them together existed only in his own head. Still when the phone rang and interrupted him at his task, it was not entirely unexpected.

"Comrade Lysenko, this is Comrade Beria. I was wondering if I could get a few moments of your precious time."

"I am always at your disposal, Comrade Beria."

"As you may know, Comrade Malenkov has reappointed me to my old post as Minister for Internal Affairs."

"I was not aware, Comrade Beria...I mean, Comrade Minister Beria...but if there is anything a humble scientist can do to support your crucial work, you need only ask."

"I'm so very glad to hear you say that. I am a good judge of character, if I may say so, and your trustworthiness and discretion is something that others might emulate."

"You are too kind."

"I shall be down to your office in a few minutes. This will be a private conversation."

"I will be eagerly awaiting your arrival."

Comrade Lysenko, alone in his office, smiled. Comrade Stalin might be dead, but his own position as the most favored scientist in the Soviet Union remained as secure as ever. One thing he knew for sure though. When next came the opportunity to perfect his grafting techniques on human subjects, he was going to make sure the windows remained locked.

What historical period did you choose and what attracted you to it?
The time period is late Stalinist Russia. The engine for the story is the bogus science of Trofim Lysenko, who believed that genetically new species of plants could be created through grafting. In our current age where politicians deny scientific reality (e.g., climate change), I wanted to explore what might happen if scientific truth actually could be ordered by government fiat.

What did you change and what do you see the fallout from it to be?
Lysenko was an agrobiologist and his focus was on crops like winter wheat. In the story his patron Stalin wants him to apply his grafting theories to humans as a means of making Stalin immortal.

Which texts were crucial to your research?
I'm afraid my research was only skin deep, relying on what's on the 'net, although there are numerous books on Lysenko, lysenkoism, and the devastatingly negative impact this bogus science had. What I needed to flesh out the story were the names and titles of Stalin's top people who would have been in on the proceedings of the story. For example, Lavrenti Beria was, indeed, the feared head of the NKVD (a precursor to the KGB and the modern FSB). One got on his bad side at their peril.

What is a good introduction to this period?
A very interesting view of Stalin and the people around him is the 1970 book *Khrushchev Remembers,* the memoir of the man who ultimately succeed him to power.

early 1980s

HIGHWAY 16
Caitlin Marceau

He holds the wheel firmly in one hand and adjusts the brim of his Stetson with the other. The leather is old and worn, worked in by use and constant wear. Even though he bought the hat in Alberta, he swears the cowhide smells like Texas. The radio plays one of his favourite country songs and he turns it up, drowning out the sound of the rain and bobbing his head in time with the music. He hums halfheartedly along with the tune, his gravel voice ripping the song to shreds in his mouth as he scans the road for signs of life.

His heater makes a long whining sound and stops pumping out hot air. The window begins to fog up, grey slowly creeping into his line of sight on the bug-smeared window. He grunts in frustration and slams his hand onto the dash. The heater gives an exhausted metal groan and turns back on, filling the pickup truck's cabin with heat once more.

He presses his foot down hard on the gas pedal and flies down Highway 16, drumming his hands on the wheel in time with the music. The rain comes down in sheets, the windshield wipers having a hard time keeping up with the falling water. He navigates his truck around a bend, grimacing as the truck slides around the turn on the wet asphalt. He steadies his Ford and continues to drive towards Prince George.

Another song begins to play but the signal's bad. The guitar and banjo twangs mix with the static and falling water to make an unpleasant melody. He reaches out a hand to shut off the radio and—with some alarm—watches as sunspots erupt across his skin. He stares as the skin on the back of his hand grows loose and wrinkled, his nails beginning to to yellow.

The car begins to rattle and shake, and he turns his attention back to the road. He steers himself off the dirt shoulder and back onto the highway. He glances back at his hands—so much older now—and grabs the pair of lambskin gloves off the passenger seat. He pulls them on without looking, eyes focused on the road, the music still blaring.

Eventually, once he's found the courage, he glances at the time on the radio.

9:48 pm.

His breath catches in his throat as he continues down the highway. He hadn't realized it was already so late, that it was already the final day of the cycle, or that he'd need to find another one so soon.

He keeps his course along the road, taking the turns slower as his vision begins to worsen. After a couple of kilometers he finally pops open the glove compartment and takes out his glasses. They're old and black rimmed, the lenses scratched and dirty. He braces the steering wheel with his knee and cleans them with the hem of his shirt. Once they're as spotless as they're going to get, he puts them on and takes the wheel once more.

He continues down Highway 16, passing an exit for a truck stop along the way. He doesn't see the sign—thick rain and bad vision keeping it hidden—and he drives right by it, his tank less than an eighth full.

His stomach growls and he immediately regrets skipping out on supper. He reaches around to the passenger's side, rifling through the piles of old clothing and random objects on the leather seat. He feels around until he finds a stale packet of Beer Nuts, and tries to rip it open with his teeth. His hands shake and the effort of pulling the wrapper open sends sharp jolts of pain shooting into his gums. He drops the snack and grunts in frustration.

The light for the gas flicks to life and he beats his hand against the steering wheel, accidentally honking the horn. He continues down the road for another twenty kilometers before the pickup truck finally crawls to a halt by the side of the highway.

He lies his head on the wheel and closes his eyes, exhaustion flooding him and dread pumping through his veins. He sits silently in the cabin, the music filling the space around him. The noise in the cramped quarters make him feel claustrophobic and when he can't take it anymore he shuts the music off. He opens the visor and reluctantly checks himself in the small mirror.

His teeth are yellow and stained, his face lined with deep wrinkles, his golden hair now ash white. What used to be a strong square jaw is now saggy skin and jowls.

But his eyes…

His eyes never change. Even when he's young his eyes stay old. He's seen and done too much in the hundreds of years he's been alive for his eyes not to show it.

He turns off the car, making sure only his hazard lights are on, and takes the key out of the ignition. He grabs his dark leather jacket and exits the Ford. He pulls on the coat—body cracking with age—and zips it closed before he gets completely drenched. He pulls his collar tight around his neck and adjusts his hat, a few stray droplets of water finding their way past the leather and rolling down his spine. It sends a chill through his bones, the arthritis he didn't have an hour ago beginning to flare up.

Locking the doors of the black pickup he begins walking down the highway, back the way he came. He walks slowly, shuffling along the side of the road. His shoulders are hunched over and his back is throbbing.

He can't help but note the irony that he's going to die on this highway. Of all the places and all the ways, he can't help but laugh that it's here his heart is finally going to give out.

He keeps walking, body shaking and fingers numb. The rain beats him down, his steps getting slower and more painful. His pants are drenched from the heavy rainfall, the water rolling down his pale legs and soaking the insides of his cowboy boots.

A bright light flashes in the distance and he closes his eyes tight, raising a hand to shield them from the brightness. He braces himself and waits for the impact, counting down the seconds until he hears the inevitable screech of brakes from a car stopping much too late.

But it never comes.

The vehicle gradually comes to a stop a few feet away from him and the driver shuts off the lights. He lowers his hand, blinking quickly to clear the spots from his vision, and his heart begins to pound fast as he hears a car door open and slam shut. Someone runs towards him and he smiles to himself as he hears an umbrella popping open.

"Sir? Sir?" a woman calls over the rain. "Are you okay?"

The woman comes towards him and holds the umbrella over his head, shielding him from the rain. He nods his head and shivers, exaggerating the movements so she sees them in the dark.

"Sir, are you sure you're okay?"

After a moment he eventually shakes his head.

"My car...It ran out of gas and I don't have a cell phone. I must have missed the sign for the gas station and now I'm all turned around," he says through chattering teeth. "I'm so sorry, but could you point me in the right direction?"

"Of course. It's down the road," she tells him, pointing in the direction of his pickup, "for another thirty kilometers and then you take the exit, continue for another three, and you can't miss it."

His face falls and he nods.

"Thank you dear," he says in the most melancholic voice he can muster. "I appreciate your help."

He smiles at her, turns around—wobbling a bit for effect—and starts heading down the highway the way he came.

It takes a few minutes longer than he'd expected, but the woman comes running up to him and shielding him with the umbrella once more.

"Sir, if you like, I can take you," she offers.

"No, no," he says quickly, "I can make it. I'll be fine."

"With all due respect, it's a long walk there and an even longer one back if you're going to be hauling fuel with you. It'll take you all night at the rate you're going. Please, let me help you."

He nods his head slowly with fake reluctance. She hands him the umbrella and runs back to her small car, starts it up, and pulls up beside the old man. She runs back out and takes the umbrella from the man and holds it over him as he gets himself into the car, pulling one cramped leg in at a time. She throws the soaking wet umbrella onto the backseat before running around to her side—yet again—and getting in.

The pair drive down the dark highway and pass his truck parked on the shoulder, lights flashing dimly.

"Is that yours?"

"Mhmm."

"It's such a big truck for such a small man! Don't your knees hurt getting in?" she asks.

"They do now, but they haven't always given me such a hard time. It feels like only yesterday that I was a much younger man," he chuckles.

"Time has a way of sneaking up on people."

He glances at the clock—11:17 pm—and nods.

"Yes, it does."

They drive the rest of the way in comfortable silence. She keeps her eyes glued to the road while he watches her from under the brim of his hat.

She's objectively beautiful: high cheekbones, copper skin, long black hair, and brown eyes that shine faintly in the light of the dashboard. He can't help but wonder how brightly they reflect the moon and stars on a clear summer night. She has full lips and a strong nose, but her chin is soft and round with only the hint of a cleft. He can't help but admire her beauty.

It's a kind he's fallen in love with over and over again for generations.

She turns her flasher on, even though no one's behind them on the road, and takes the exit off Highway 16. He stares as lights become visible through the rain in the distance.

"It's so different," he mutters to himself.

"Oh?"

"This area used to be nothing but forest," he tells her as she pulls up to one of the gas pumps, shutting off the car. "There was nothing but trees and wild animals."

She laughs politely and shakes her head.

"You must be thinking of somewhere else. This area's been developed since before I was born. My grandparents used to complain about how the nearby town was always expanding."

"Trees and wildlife," he says with a raised voice, "that's all that used to be here. When I came over from England they'd just begun to settle this area. It was an interesting time to be alive. Everything felt...new."

The woman shifts in her seat and her voice sounds too high when she speaks.

"Sir, I think you're getting yourself mixed up. Too many history books, and age can be cruel. My grandmother used to have problems with that."

"I'm not mixed up, you stupid bitch. I traveled to Fort St. James from London. They promised us all a better life and a world of possibilities." he says, staring at his reflection in the window of the car door.

He looks like he's in his eighties now, his hair thin and missing along his crown, sunspots marking his face. Deep bags hang under his cold green eyes and his lips are thin and reptilian. He looks away, disgusted.

"I didn't want to come here," he explains. His voice is rough and steady, all traces of confusion and fear gone. "I wanted to stay in London, but people—my family—were starting to notice how...unchanging I was. I needed to start all over again."

The woman leans away from him—eyes darting between the man beside her and the light coming from the inside of the service station—and places one hand on her belt buckle and the other on the handle of her door.

"Sorry," he says, "I think you're right; I'm not feeling myself. Between the rain and the long walk, I've had a terrible night. I'm so sorry, dear." He covers his face with a hand and shakes his head. "I sound absolutely crazy, don't I? Oh Lord, I've turned into my grandfather. I'm so sorry if I've made you uncomfortable."

"Don't worry about it. You've been through a lot tonight," she says fast, pulling the door handle and turning her attention to the light across the gas station platform.

As she looks away, he takes off one of his lambskin gloves and, as she turns back, he places his bare hand to the side of her face. The touch sends a chill running through her skin, rippling through her body from the point of contact. She tries to move, but finds herself unable. She tries to scream, but her mouth only hangs open in a silent "O".

"I really am sorry," he says, voice anything but sincere, "but I didn't know the other girl was sick. I didn't know she had so little time to borrow."

He smiles as the sunspots and wrinkles fade from his skin. His hair grows back thick—white strands turning into golden waves—and his hanging jowls tighten back into a strong jawline. Arthritic and stiff joints find release, his hunched back straightening out, and his eyesight comes back sharper than before. She watches transfixed, even as her sight begins to dull, as the eighty year-old changes to a young man.

Her breathing slows, each inhale a strain on her body. She can feel her blood pumping at a snail's pace through her veins as panic floods her senses. She feels like she's drowning in slow motion as her body begins to shut down one part at a time, twitching and writhing until it's still and all that's left alive is her mind—thoughts swirling in terror and fury at her own death. Soon, the synapses in her brain stop firing and she's still.

The man removes his palm from her face and licks her sweat from his hand. He opens and closes his hand, admiring the way taut muscles moves under the healthy skin, and tries to shake the pins and needles from his arm. It's the same unpleasant sensation every time he drains someone. Still, remembering his aged reflection in the window of the car, he knows it could be worse.

It almost was.

He fixes his clothing, arranging it to hang properly on his sturdy form, and pulls his glove back on. He gets out of the car and reaches through to the driver's seat, pulling the woman's lifeless body onto the empty chair. It takes some effort to move her body and she sits awkwardly in the seat, limbs bent at uncomfortable angles. He arranges her to look as normal as possible, and closes the door.

He crosses the empty lot to the service centre. The employee behind the counter is staring down at his phone, laughing at something on the screen, and doesn't bother to look up as the man roams the aisles. He grabs a bag of chips and a plastic gas canister, then brings them to the register.

The gas station attendant pauses his video and looks up, stifling a yawn.

"Find everything?"

"Mhmm." the man says, pulling out a few bills from his wallet and pointing to the car in the lot. "Can you add fifty bucks for gas."

The employee nods and rings up the total. He takes the money from the man's gloved hand and gives him back his change.

"Safe driving, eh? It's pretty bad out there."

The man smiles, pocketing the remainder of his cash.

"I think the worst is behind us."

He grabs his stuff off the counter, tips his hat to the kid in thanks, and walks back out to the car.

He opens the passenger door, tosses his snack on top of the dead woman, and slams the door shut before turning his attention to the gas pump. He takes the nozzle and puts it into the bright orange container, filling it to the brim. He puts the nozzle back on the pump, places the container on the floor of the passenger's seat, and climbs into the driver's side. He adjusts the seat, the mirrors, and arranges the steering wheel so it's not pressing into his knees before making his way back onto Highway 16.

About halfway to his truck the man pulls the car over, gets out and walks to the woman's side. He throws his food onto the dashboard and grabs the body by the hair, pulling her out of the car. Her body falls onto the shoulder of the road and she watches with wide empty eyes as he grabs the back of her jacket and drags her through the mud to the edge of the ditch that borders the gravel strip and kicks her in. The aboriginal woman watches as he drives away in her car, staring after him long after he's gone.

Once he gets to his black truck he dumps the gas into the tank and hops into the cab of the Ford. He leaves the woman's car unlocked and running, not bothering to shut it off before continuing on to Prince George.

As the rain finally begins to stop, he can't help but wonder if they'll find her come morning. If someone will see her body— cold and alone—begging to be found like the others were, or if the British Columbian wildlife will devour her body like they have countless others.

He looks at the glowing green clock—smiling for the first time in days at how much time he now has—and blasts the radio as he flies down Highway 16, heading home.

What historical period did you choose and what attracted you to it?
The '80s are making a huge comeback, specifically its aesthetic, but people are quick to forget the tragedies that took place during this time. On Highway 16, on a stretch of road known at the Highway of Tears, aboriginal women have been going missing since 1969. I thought it would be both an interesting concept to give these abductions an alternate history to them, but also highlight the need for justice for missing and murdered aboriginal women in Canada.

What did you change and what do you see the fallout from it to be?
I added a supernatural element to the abductions and murder of women on the Highway of Tears, giving the attacker a backstory that puts him in B.C. and Alberta during its initial colonization.

Which texts were crucial to your research?
News reports concerning the missing women, as well as articles and thought pieces on violence towards Native American women in Canada.

What is a good introduction to this period?
Definitely read *Dry Lips Oughta Move to Kapuskasing* by Tomson Highway. Not only is it a great look at the '80s aesthetic I based the story on, but it's a beautiful and insightful play centering around hockey and taking place on a Canadian reservation.

unfixed in time, revisited

UNKNOWN POSSIBILITIES
David Hoenig

Cassiopeia Deluxe looked at the sleek lines of the metal cabin resting on the ground, then to the lines leading to the inflatable bag above, and whistled an appreciative cat-call. She caressed its smooth wall with a gloved hand, then grinned at the older man beside her. "The 'Roo is a real beauty, isn't she Professor?"

Manfred Clutzenpfeffer didn't look up from the manifest he was examining, and when he spoke, his voice was polite and very precise. "It's a dirigible, Miss Deluxe. A thing engineered—albeit brilliantly, I may modestly add—from base materials for an express purpose. That it was named for its task of hopping from island to island to investigate the lands around us is due to the vagaries of democratic demagoguery and a perhaps dubious appreciation of puns." He looked over his half-glasses at her. "Besides, it could hardly be sexed, regardless of any particular aesthetic appeal, hmm?"

"Don't be such a literal-minded killjoy, Professor." Cassiopeia was young, tall, and lithe, her Ethiopian heritage clearly defined by the color of her skin and the bones of her face. Her teeth were very white when she smiled at him. "'Aesthetic appeal' aside; when do we finally board her and go exploring?"

Clutzenpfeffer tapped the manifest. "Two mornings hence. Think of it—thirty six years…"

"And change."

The Professor nodded. "And change, as you say, since the Big Shuffle. Most of that was figuring out what we still had here in this hodge-podge of Sydney, establishing a new government and laws, and a society which could integrate all of the people who ended up here."

She smiled, and put her arm through his and pulled him with her as she began to circle the gondola. "Like backward you, from the late nineteenth."

"And insouciant, overly-forward you, born nearly twenty years after the 'cards' were newly dealt, my dear. I must say, I've enjoyed watching you excel in your military training almost as much as our friendship and conversations."

Cassiopeia impulsively kissed his cheek. "And I appreciate all your support in getting me onto this mission."

"Think nothing of it. You've worked terribly hard for this. Besides, I'll feel safer knowing I have your uncanny accuracy and medic's training to rely upon."

She chuckled briefly, then sighed. "The only thing which would make it sweeter is if my parents had seen this day."

Clutzenpfeffer looked at her fondly. "I know they would be extremely proud." He looked around. "They would be of all we've achieved. In large part, it was the effort and sacrifice that they and so many others made that have brought us to this momentous point. Given that it's only been a handful of years since we've solidified the defenses, recreated a modicum of industry beyond subsistence, and established a reasonably secure life here in Shuffled Sydney, it would be fair to even use the word 'remarkable'."

Cassiopeia nodded as they returned to their starting point. "So. Enough with the history lesson, Professor. When do we get to go? And where?"

"Since our test flights have gathered information all along the Australian coast, it's been decided that we will check our northern neighbor, New Guinea, and see how the Shuffle acted there. Councilor Fitzroy wants to leave tomorrow, and..."

"No! Fitz 'the Pits' is coming with us?"

Clutzenpfeffer patted Cassiopeia on the arm reassuringly. "The Council is underwriting this exploration, and if we make contact with any neighbors he will have the authority to treat with them. Besides, he helped your parents conceive of and design this dirigible."

"You worked on it, too. Why aren't just you and I enough?"

"I may have participated in the overall concept, yes, but its technology is far beyond my time, my dear. If we run into any mechanical issues it would be best to have a competent engineer and pilot with us. Besides, the councilor was the first volunteer for the mission, very vociferous in his desire to take on this responsibility. Said something about New Guinea having been part of the territory of Australia during his life pre-change."

"He won't be any help if there's violence, not in his wheelchair. I think it's foolish..."

The Professor interrupted her discourse. "It may be of some risk, but it's hardly foolish. His mobility might be an issue, but the vessel is outfitted with a swivel-gun which can be deployed and operated from the helm in the event of hostilities, and that will be his primary station on our journey. Now, why has he earned his sobriquet?"

"His what?"

"What does 'the Pits' mean, my dear?"

She bit her lip. "It's not complimentary." At his raised eyebrow, she continued with some reluctance. "Well, he has antiquated notions about women."

"Seems fitting, since he's from a—how did he put it?—a 'cold war-era' version of Australia and served in 'Pine Gap' before relocating to Sydney, perhaps eighty or more years earlier than your own?"

"But you don't treat women the way he does, Professor, and you're from farther back in time."

"True. But before you speak too badly of the man, recall that he also selected you based on you heading the list of combat specialists."

She squinted at him. "Are you saying I owe him?"

"I'm saying that he knows your worth, my dear, and your parents thought well enough of him to count him a friend. Other than that, I'm afraid that all I can say is that he'll be useful, and, as the Council has insisted upon his inclusion, necessary."

Cassiopeia met his gaze, then finally dropped it and nodded her acceptance.

Clutzenpfeffer removed her arm from his gently, but held her hand for an extra moment. "Be assured that I'm ecstatic to have you along, my dear. Nowhere else in this scrambled and reassembled puzzle of Earth could I find a more delightful travelling companion, Miss Deluxe, who is as skilled as you are at killing with such a wide variety of weapons."

The woman smiled widely, and her white teeth once again shone brightly against her dark skin. "Well, I will say this Professor—you always know just how to sweet-talk a girl."

The next morning dawned clear, and Cassiopeia, Professor Clutzenpfeffer, and Councilor Hugh Fitzroy were in the control room of the 'Roo after what turned out to be only a short round of speechmaking and wishes for success. Fitzroy, sat in his rolling chair at the pilot's station, manipulated the controls to take them north away from the crowd as they gained altitude. "Most of that lot were there for the free food and beer rather than to see us go, you know."

Cassiopeia stood behind the Professor, who was in the copilot's seat. "Maybe it was less about seeing us go than about seeing you go, Councilor."

Clutzenpfeffer gave her a sharp look, but Fitzroy only chuckled. "Fair dinkum, ducky. Nice to see you can dish it too—makes you even more interesting, it does. Now, why don't you bring us a bottle of whiskey to celebrate a bit for ourselves?"

The Professor cleared his throat before Cassiopeia could retort. When he spoke, it was in his usual precise tones. "Councilor, Miss Deluxe was selected for her ability with firearms and hand to hand combat, not to mention her fluency in four languages and training as a medic, not to…"

"Save it, Professor. He knows all that—he's just baiting me."

"Now would I do that, ducky?"

She ignored him. "I didn't even know we had alcohol on board."

Clutzenpfeffer sniffed. "Since the Shuffle may have left literally anyone anywhere, we don't have any idea whom we'll be meeting. Ethanol is a valuable trade commodity in a majority of human societies throughout history, so the Councilor and I made sure we had some aboard."

"Yes indeed," Fitzroy agreed. "But, as a result I'm afraid the party might end a bit earlier for those bogans back there…when you consider exactly how much I lifted from the Council's stock."

Cassiopeia laughed despite herself at the unflattering slang description of the crowd. "Okay, fine, you win. You two keep flying this thing, I'll find the whiskey."

"It'll be in the 'Medicinal Supplies' cabinet."

"And, of course it is." The men chuckled as she left to find it, and upon her return they shared out glasses.

The Councilor held his up for a toast. "To a successful first mission." They all drank.

Savoring the taste, Cassiopeia watched the dirigible's progress over the coastline below. "You know something Fitzroy?"

"Hmm?"

"Pretty slick of you to heist the whiskey. Maybe you're not quite the arsehole everyone says you are."

The Councilor turned back to her with a wry smile. "Or maybe it's just that I'm your kind of arsehole, ducky."

It made her laugh. "Maybe that," she agreed, then poured out another shot for them all.

There was some excitement as they left land behind to cross the ocean between them and New Guinea, but that paled quickly in the unrelieved scenery below. Clutzenpfeffer took his turn at the helm, and insisted that Cassiopeia learn the basic controls as well, which she did. Later, they put the ship on autopilot to share meals in the main cabin, and afterwards they took turns sleeping and flying.

When dawn came the following morning, Cassiopeia looked out the main cabin windows after waking and saw land below and ahead of them. "We're there already?"

The Professor was writing in a journal and glanced out, then at his watch. "Our top cruising speed is impressive by late nineteenth standards: nearly sixty miles per hour. Since it's roughly seventeen hundred miles from Sydney to Papua, it should take just under thirty hours to reach where the old maps put Papua's airport."

"So, what you're saying is…?"

"Yes, Miss Deluxe—we're there already. Or, more precisely, almost."

She smiled. "What's the plan for the day?" She picked up the telescope which sat upon the table and peered through it out the window.

"Observations, to begin with. We'll stay high enough so we're not within easy reach of the ground in case there's any hostile action by anything from dinosaurs to attack aircraft. I want to check the geography of the island, see if there are any anomalies dealt in by the Shuffle, like that desert that ended up to the west of Sydney."

After a moment, she murmured, as if to herself. "Well, isn't that strange?"

Clutzenpfeffer kept writing without looking up. "Isn't what strange, Miss Deluxe?"

"That mountain, sitting all by itself like that in the middle of the rainforest."

The Professor set down his journal and pen and stood up carefully. He took the telescope and peered along the line that Cassiopeia pointed. "Well. That is fascinating, isn't it?"

"I thought the mountainous spine of New Guinea ran east-west, Professor."

"It does, my dear. And there are no mountains along the Fly River's course south of it; at least, there were not before the Shuffle." He handed her the telescope. "I believe I will ask Councilor Fitzroy to take us in that direction." Clutzenpfeffer hesitated before he went into the cockpit, and turned back to her with a broad smile. "Well done, my dear."

It took another two hours to reach the coast where the river emptied into the bay, and they followed the waterway inland at an altitude of several hundred feet. Nowhere did they see any sign of industrial presence, though they did observe movement in the open spaces between the trees, creatures which appeared both startled and agitated by the dirigible's passage above them but of whom the explorers could not obtain a clear view.

Finally, Fitzroy cleared his throat. "I once flew over New Guinea in the 1960's, pre-Shuffle, of course. They'd discovered copper in Bougainville and started a major mine there. I remember villages and towns all over, but I've seen nothing so far except native forest."

Clutzenpfeffer nodded. "There's been no sign of any technology at all. Of course, before the end of the 16th century, there was no recorded intrusions, Hugh. Still, I'd have expected to see at least some human presence below us, not that we've observed much of the land, percentage-wise. Any natives could be from any century of their pre-colonial era, I would judge."

"I'll agree with you that far, but from up here it looks like nearly primordial jungle. I'd love to go down for some close observation and sampling of the leaves and wildlife."

From her position doing core exercises on the floor of the main cabin, Cassiopeia answered. "Not a good idea for several reasons, gentlemen. For one, there's no landing site, so we would have to rappel from the cabin without prior surveillance of the terrain beneath the tree canopy. Virtually anything could be down there, and anything includes a frightening array of lethal possibilities. Instead, I'd strongly recommend we head to the mountain and check it out, as it's the only anomalous terrain with clearance to inspect and land. It must be worth the trip, right?"

The Professor smiled. "Sound logic, Miss Deluxe. Hugh—how much longer would you estimate until we reach it?"

"Perhaps two more hours. You're sure you don't want to make a try for the jungle below, Manfred?"

Despite the strenuous exercise, Cassiopeia's voice carried no strain when she answered Fitzroy's question. "If we're in pre-colonial New Guinea, any people down there are almost certainly cannibals, Councilor, there were and are a whole variety of dangerous native wildlife, and neither possibility takes into account any wild predators which might have been dealt here by the Shuffle."

"But…"

"Let me be blunt: any way you look at it, you'd be steak on the hoof, Fitz."

The Councilor glared at her for a moment, then maneuvered his chair to the control room without another word. Clutzenpfeffer gave her a disapproving look.

Cassiopeia raised one eyebrow at him. "What? Down there, any of us might be."

"That's true, but hardly civil of you to be so blunt with him."

"Professor, one of the reasons you brought me was to keep the unknown possibilities for death and disaster to the absolute minimum."

Clutzenpfeffer didn't respond except for a grunt of grudging assent before returning to his writing.

A little over two hours later, all three were in the control room and Fitzroy was again piloting. The dirigible had gained additional altitude to be able to inspect the out-of-place mountain from above. Fitzroy pointed out the forward window. "It's a plateau."

The Professor had the telescope. "It's built like a stone fortress. And it's inhabited—and they've seen us."

"Weapons?" Cassiopeia stood behind the men, dressed in brown fatigues.

"I see metal blades, spears, shields."

"Missile weapons besides the spears?"

"Nothing… No, wait. I see at least one bow. But their main force looks to be engaged at the edge of where the trees give way just below the level ground we can see."

"They're in the middle of a fight? With whom?"

"Looks that way, but I can't see."

Fitzroy glanced at the Professor. "Want me to circle around?"

"Yes Councilor, please do. I'm looking for any clues…Oh. Well that's interesting."

Cassiopeia tightened her grip on the back of the copilot's chair. "What?"

"They appear to have darker skin than me or Hugh, far lighter than yours. And I believe they're wearing skullcaps, Miss Deluxe."

"What does that mean?"

Fitzroy banged his hand against his console, making the other two jump. "This is just ripper! Absolutely spectacular!"

Clutzenpfeffer peered at him. "Care to enlighten us, Councilor?"

"What do a mountain plateau with stone fortress, sword and bow technology, and skullcaps on the residents add up to in light of the event which so scrambled our world?"

The Professor broke into a smile. "Oh. Oh, how marvelous! We must make landing preparations immediately."

"Wait, you've both lost me," Cassiopeia complained. "Who are these folk?"

"Well, it looks like the Shuffle dealt a pretty strange hand here, ducky," Fitzroy said. He eased back on the throttle and brought the airship to a relative halt about fifty feet above and south of the plateau's wall. They could see more people arriving below: men, women, and children, all of them armed. Mostly they stood, pointing and looking at the dirigible in surprise. The Councilor turned to face her. "Welcome to Masada, I think."

Cassiopeia looked at Clutzenpfeffer for an explanation.

"The Sicarii retreated to Masada when Jerusalem fell to the Romans around 70 of the Common Era—"

Fitzroy interrupted. "72 into 73."

Clutzenpfeffer ignored him. "I'd guess that the mountain was Shuffled out from ancient Israel and dropped here in the middle of Papua. Now: how's your Latin, Miss Deluxe?"

She swallowed. "Moderatus."

"Excellent. My Hebrew is a bit rusty, and may suffer from being a more modern version, but at least we'll likely have some common ground to explore. Let's radio our position and findings back to Sydney, then see if we can reassure those below that we've come in peace before we set down, eh Hugh?"

"And how exactly do you suggest we do that?"

"I believe I know just the thing."

The 'Roo was anchored to several large rocks by lines but stayed aloft. Cassiopeia looked up at the side of it where the Professor had unfurled a banner which read 'Shalom'—'Peace'. Fitzroy was on board and at the controls of both the ship and its guns, but her clenched jaw underscored her nervousness as she watched Clutzenpfeffer approach an old man at the head of a number of spear- and bow-armed men. He had grey at his temples and in his long beard, and wore threadbare robes, a skullcap, and a cloth with fringes at the corner. Cassiopeia clutched her Austeyr EF88 tightly, and let her eyes flick this way and that in order to keep the growing, milling crowd behind the man in view.

After an exchange of words between the two men in what Cassiopeia assumed was Hebrew, she caught the Professor switch to hesitant Latin and gesture in her direction. A suspicious look came across the old man's face as he looked at her, but he nodded after a moment and answered back. Though her Latin was certainly rusty, she found she understood the man easily enough.

"I am Eleazar ben Yair, leader of this community."

The Professor bowed his head respectfully. "A great honor, Rabbi. I am Manfred Clutzenpfeffer, historian and scholar, and lately an explorer. My companion here is Cassiopeia, a warrior and explorer as well."

"Greek?" Eleazar sounded surprised.

Cassiopeia answered for herself. "Only my name, Rabbi. The rest of me is Australian."

He repeated that, questioningly, and glanced at Clutzenpfeffer. "Cushi? K'Miryam, eishet Moshe?"

"What did he say, Professor?"

"He asks in Hebrew if you are Cushite—due to your dark skin, I suppose, my dear—like the wife of Moses."

"Oh." She considered for only a moment before replying in Latin. "Yes, honored Rabbi."

Clutzenpfeffer turned back to Eleazar. "Can you tell us what happened to you and your people? You are the Sicarii of Israel, yes?"

"Indeed. We had taken refuge after capturing Herod's fort on Masada, and were attacking small forces, striking the invading Romans who had sacked the great Temple in Jerusalem. Then, more than thirty-six years ago everything suddenly changed.

"We knew that the Tenth Legion had marched against us, with Flavius Silva leading it, and that our days were numbered. But as the Legion came into view and we resolved ourselves to a long siege, it seemed to us that God Himself answered our prayers for salvation.

"The heavens seemed to split, the ground roared as though the mountain were breaking free to hurl itself at our enemy, only then there was no Tenth Legion, nor Flavius Silva. There was this place, with its trees and rain—it made the plateau bloom and filled the cisterns to capacity. In the very beginning, it seemed as though we might have been taken to the Garden of Eden itself."

A cry from across the plateau resounded, and though Cassiopeia could not understand it—Hebrew again, she assumed—it seemed to galvanize the Rabbi and his people. She brought her gun part-way up to firing position. "Uh, Professor..."

"They're under attack, it seems." He spoke rapidly to the leader of the Sicarii.

"By whom? From where?" She pressed her throat microphone to activate it. "Fitz, can you see anything?"

The Councilor's voice came back loud and clear. "Not tethered to the ground, I can't. It seems to be coming from the other side of the plateau, where there's a long, snaky path down into the trees, but the cover is too heavy to see through."

Clutzenpfeffer finished speaking hurriedly with Eleazar in Hebrew, before the leader of the Sicarii turned to address a group which came running to report. "The Rabbi says they're under attack from the lowlands. If I understand him correctly, his people have been fighting defensively since shortly after the Shuffle dealt them here. Initially, they skirmished with a number of different native tribes in the jungle below, but that was only in the beginning. They were never able to threaten this mountain fortress—the Sicarii have better quality weapons and the defensible terrain in their favor—but not long after that came natives fleeing from…Well, I'm not sure of the translation."

The Rabbi finished giving instructions to a number of men and women who raced away to whatever tasks had been assigned, and turned back. "They come—I don't know why they attack now, but our scouts say many, many."

Cassiopeia glanced to the edge of the plateau but saw nothing. "By what? Quid est impetus?"

Eleazar ben Yair's lips thinned. "Vermes. Praegrandis."

The Professor looked aghast. When he spoke to Cassiopeia, it was in English. "'Gigantic vermin'? Dear god, might we have triggered this aggression?"

"What do we do, Professor?"

Fitzroy chimed in over the radio. "Here's a thought: get your asses on board and let's get back to Sydney and let these folk have their little ambit!"

Clutzenpfeffer looked torn. "But, but it may be our fault…"

"We can help them." Cassiopeia thumbed the safety off her rifle. "I'm not afraid."

The sounds of battle—cries, bow strings snapping, and weapons clashing—began to carry from the far side of the plateau. Eleazar ben Yair moved hurriedly in that direction, calling out commands.

"Now hold on, ducky," Fitzroy said over the radio. "What gives you the right to decide whom to fight for and against? This should be discussed among the Councilors before we commit to a political decision with far-reaching ramifications, let alone risking our lives in the bargain."

"But we can't just stand by and do nothing!" She rushed to Clutzenpfeffer's side and craned her neck to look towards where the defenders had amassed. Young teens at the periphery of the blade-wielding Sicarii carried bows, and were now being handed arrows by younger children too small to see over the heads of the rest. Darker skinned natives, dressed in the garb of the Masadans, formed up at the rear with spears, clearly drilled in the ancient Roman style by the Sicarii. "We have to help."

Fitzroy's voice broke in again, exasperated. "We don't even know what they're up against!"

Clutzenpfeffer looked lost, his eyes compassionate wells which tracked the first casualties being brought to the rear of the battle lines, screaming in pain. "We must do something!"

"I'll go join their lines, see what they're fighting and radio back. You and Fitz set up a triage area." She was off and running.

"Be careful, my dear!" the Professor called after her.

Cassiopeia raced to where the leader of the Sicarii and a small group of advisors stood commanding the battle. "The 'vermin'? Vermes?" she asked them.

Eleazar spoke quickly in Hebrew to one of his subordinates, a young woman with short dark hair who bore a flag in one hand, but wore a short, broad blade in her belt. The woman nodded, then looked to Cassiopeia and pointed with the flag to a position at the left side of the defensive force. She then gestured at herself. "Esther bat Avigail," then walked off at a quick pace.

Cassiopeia followed, observant of the tactics of the mixed force. Soldiers with shields and short, thrusting javelins were massed at the front, while behind them were spearmen and women who worked with precision between the defensive wall between them and the attacking force. She could see that some of those in the second rank held an oddly tipped spear; instead of a tapered point, it was more like a forked point with spikes on each inside tip.

The Sicaria motioned Cassiopeia to follow her and moved to a stone wall which bordered their side of the plateau. Two soldiers with long wooden poles with tips like that of a rake stood watching its top carefully, while the main shield rank anchored to the wall and stretched across what appeared to be the main descent from the mountain fortress.

"So, what are we up against?" Fitzroy's voice over her headphone was tense.

"Can't see yet. They've got a shield wall...Wait!" One of the fighters went to one knee to make a block, and she saw the enemy between the front ranks. For several moments though, the sight was so unexpected that she couldn't process it.

One of the fighters with the fork-tipped spear jumped forward, and as something jabbed forward into the Sicarii lines, the strange polearm caught it and pinned it to the ground. A call went up, and a warrior with an iron sword chopped down at it.

Cassiopeia caught her breath. "Giant scorpions?" she said wonderingly. Realizing she hadn't activated her microphone she did and repeated her report in a firmer voice.

The professor's voice was excited when it came over. "How large?"

She moved closer, careful of the moving fighters, and was distracted by a sudden movement to her left. A scorpion topped the wall, tail poised to strike, and the two rake-wielders shoved with their poles to push it back from the wall. She swallowed. "Looks like just under a meter."

"Amazing! Likely from the Devonian period. To think, the Shuffle dealt us something from 400 million…"

Cassiopeia tuned out as one of the fighters in the line before her went down, impaled in the shoulder. The woman with the flag—Esther, she recalled—who'd accompanied her jumped forward, sword drawn and swinging to amputate the tail. Cassiopeia followed, gun up, buttstock against her cheek and used a light pull to put several bullets into the creature in front of her. It fell, instantly dead.

The Sicarii to her right and left spared glances which showed astonished faces. Esther bat Avigail seemed less concerned about the strange weapon's noise than about what it could do, and began to shout orders as she took tactical control of the front line. She gestured with her flag and warriors shifted to provide lines of sight for Cassiopeia to fire into the advancing scorpions. A spearman grabbed the fighter who'd been stung and dragged him backwards, away from the battle line.

The Austeyr 88 changed the battle entirely, and with Cassiopeia's firepower and the Sicaria's leadership, they were even able to advance down the path. The scorpions fell, came, fell, and finally were gone. Not another defender was injured, and the fighting force let out a collective victory cry.

The professor's voice came over her headset. "I presume we've won, Miss Deluxe?"

"We're clear up here, Professor." She saw warriors reestablish a perimeter, while others began to amputate the tails of their enemy, and drag carcasses back into the fortress. "Oh!"

"What's wrong?"

"Nothing. I just had a mildly nauseous moment."

Fitzroy intruded, the smile clear in his words. "Really? Bloodshed getting to you, ducky?"

Cassiopeia slapped a fresh clip into her rifle, and scanned the woods ahead. "No, Fitz. Just what's likely to be on the menu tonight."

"Practical," the professor mused.

"Bleh," Fitzroy contributed.

Esther bat Avigail gave a signal which brought the warriors back, except for scouts. Cassiopeia chuckled. "I'll see if I can get us an invitation to dinner, Councilor."

The casualties were resting inside the fortress, having received what first aid the crew of the 'Roo could offer.

Fiztroy sat in his chair in the doorway of the airship and watched his companions speaking with the leader of the Sicarii, Eleazar ben Yair, opening negotiations which they would take back to Sydney and the Council. He looked to his right to see the canvas that Clutzenpfeffer had unfurled along the cabin's side, with its message: Shalom, and a smile grew on his face.

"Not bad for a first mission, I'd say."

Cassiopeia must have overheard him speak but not precisely what, because she looked a question in his direction as the professor and the Rabbi continued to speak. He waved her over, and she excused herself before moving in his direction.

"What?" she asked when she arrived at the 'Roo.

"How'd the scorpion steak taste?" He laughed when she wrinkled her nose, and again when she looked annoyed at him. "I'm kidding; I said we did pretty good work here. I'm glad you were with us, Cassiopeia." He held out a fresh bottle of whiskey for her.

The smile she gave him was full of joy as she accepted the bottle and took a swig.

"Now, if we can only pry Clutzenpfeffer away from living history, we can head home. See what you can do about that, eh, ducky?"

What historical period did you choose and what attracted you to it?

I wanted a modern take on dirigible exploration, but with the world and times reshuffled. This gave me the opportunity to put modern folk with those from the Victorian age and cold war era, and have them explore a jungle environment with transplanted ancient Israelis from the time of the Roman Empire's occupation. The realization that people from such disparate backgrounds, geographies, social situations, and religions, could all come to a point of peace and harmony in a new era was very attractive and rewarding to write about.

What did you change and what do you see the fallout from it to be?

I changed geography, social structures, and tossed it all together into a mix. The fallout is a nucleus of civilization where "the other" is neither feared nor hated, but rather a difference worthy of exploration and understanding.

What texts were crucial to your research?

I used geographical texts and maps of Australia and New Guinea, consulted stories about Masada (including translations of Josephus' descriptions of the Roman assault), and personal accounts of studies of the Aboriginal groups of New Guinea.

What is a good introduction to this period?

Regarding the cannibalism in New Guinea, this interview with Paul Raffaele informed some of the story: **vice.com/en_us/article/qbe55p/hanging-out-with-cannibals-georgia-rose-377**

Regarding Masada, much has been written, but this translation of Josephus Flavius is informative: **pbs.org/wgbh/pages/frontline/shows/religion/maps/primary/josephusmasada.html**. Also, historical description: **timesofisrael.com/masada-tragic-fortress-in-the-sky/**

AUTHOR BIOS

Patrick S. Baker

Patrick S. Baker is a U.S. Army Veteran, currently a Department of Defense employee. He has advanced degrees in History and Political Science. His nonfiction has appeared in *Strategy and Tactics* and *Modern Warfare.* His fiction has appeared in *Astounding Frontiers* and *Mythic Magazine* as well as the *Uncommon Minds* and *After Avalon* anthologies, among others. In his spare time he reads, works out, plays war-games, and enjoys life with his wife and dog.

Stewart C. Baker

Stewart C Baker is an academic librarian, SFF author and poet, and haikuist. His fiction has appeared in *Writers of the Future, Nature,* and *Galaxy's Edge,* among other places. Stewart was born in England, has lived in South Carolina, Japan, and California (in that order), and currently resides in Oregon with his family—although if anyone asks, he'll usually say he's from the internet.

Russell Hemmell

Russell Hemmell is a statistician and social scientist from the U.K, passionate about astrophysics and speculative fiction. Recent work in *Helios Quarterly Magazine, Not One of Us, Perihelion SF,* and others. Finalist in The Canopus 100 Year Starship Awards 2016-2017.'

David M. Hoenig

David is a practicing surgeon who lives to write, rather than writing to live. He is helped in this endeavor by his wife and hindered by his cats, but is extremely grateful for both. His website of publications can be found at: **davidmhoenig.wordpress.com/about/**

Anne E. Johnson

Anne E. Johnson is a Brooklyn-based writer of all sorts of things. Nearly a hundred of her short stories, mostly in the science fiction and fantasy genres, have been published in a variety of magazines and anthologies. She also writes arts journalism, including two regular columns about music for PS Audio's *Copper Magazine* and occasional pieces for *Classical Voice North America* and *Early Music America.*

Daniel M. Kimmel

Daniel M. Kimmel is the author of Hugo finalist *Jar Jar Binks Must Die,* a collection of essays on SF movies, and a growing number of short stories and novels marked by his twisted sense of humor. His most recent was *Time on My Hands,* a send up of the cliches of time travel stories. He is currently working on *Father of the Bride of Frankenstein* combining two popular subjects: weddings and reanimated corpses.

Caitlin Marceau

Caitlin Marceau is an author and professional editor living and working in Montreal. She holds a B.A. in Creative Writing, is a member of the Horror Writers Association, and has spoken about horror literature and media at several Canadian conventions. Her first coauthored collection, *Read-Only: A Collection of Digital Horror,* was published in 2017. For more information or check out her work, visit **caitlinmarceau.com**.

Eugene Morgulis

Eugene Morgulis was born in Kiev, raised in Milwaukee, schooled in Boston, and now lives in Los Angeles. He writes speculative fiction and practices law in the fields of data privacy and cybersecurity. Read more of his work at **eugenemorgulis. com/writing**.

Caroline Sciriha

Caroline Sciriha lives in Malta, where she works as a Head of Department of English in a State Secondary School. She writes fiction—especially fantasy—whenever her day job allows. Her work has appeared in various anthologies and magazines including *Childhood Regained, New Myths and Memories of the Past: 2016 Anthology*.

Alex Shvartsman

Alex Shvartsman is a writer, translator and game designer from Brooklyn, NY. Over 100 of his short stories have appeared in *Nature, Galaxy's Edge, InterGalactic Medicine Show,* and many other magazines and anthologies. He won the 2014 WSFA Small Press Award for Short Fiction and was a two-time finalist for the Canopus Award for Excellence in Interstellar Fiction (2015 and 2017). He is the editor of the *Unidentified Funny Objects* annual anthology series of humorous SF/F. His latest collection, *The Golem of Deneb Seven and Other Stories,* is forthcoming in 2018. His website is **alexshvartsman.com**.

Nemma Wollenfang

Nemma Wollenfang is an MSc Postgraduate and prize-winning short story writer who lives in Northern England. Her work has appeared in several venues, including three of Flame

Tree's bestselling Gothic Fantasy hardbacks: *Science Fiction Short Stories, Murder Mayhem* and *Pirates & Ghosts*. She can be found on facebook, goodreads and twitter: @NemmaW.

EDITOR BIOS

Joseph Cadotte

Joseph is a game designer and lead editor at his family's educational software company, Innovative Learning Solutions. He also founded Old Sins as a literary cooperative and an alternative to many mainstream presses. Joseph has authored two novels and one graphic novel, all hard science fiction, with more on the way. He lives in the lovely resort town of Wilmington, NC with his dog, Dwight "Doggie" Eisenhower, his cat, Ophelia, his wife, Cordelia, and their son, Jacob.

Elizabeth Kidder

Elizabeth Kidder is an author and illustrator, working in both fields for over half a dozen years. Previous publications include a selection of poems and short stories in the *Artemis* literary journal at the Savannah College of Art and Design, and her first novel, *ColorBlind,* released in 2017. When she's not working, she likes to unwind by drawing horses and hosting podcasts. She lives in Tennessee with her husband, two cats, and a collection of books that is constantly outgrowing its shelf space. You can view her work at **elizabethkidder.com**.